THE WORKS OF
HENRY VAN DYKE
AVALON EDITION
VOLUME III

౭

OUTDOOR ESSAYS

III

From a painting by Frank E. Schoonover

Chichester followed along the open shore

DAYS OFF

AND OTHER DIGRESSIONS

BY

HENRY VAN DYKE

I do not count the hours I spend
In wandering by the sea;
The forest is my loyal friend,
Like God it useth me:

Or on the mountain-crest sublime,
Or down the oaken glade,
O what have I to do with Time?
For this the day was made.
—RALPH WALDO EMERSON.

NEW YORK
CHARLES SCRIBNER'S SONS
1920

To

MY FRIEND AND NEIGHBOUR
GROVER CLEVELAND
WHOSE YEARS OF GREAT WORK
AS A STATESMAN
HAVE BEEN CHEERED BY DAYS OF GOOD PLAY
AS A FISHERMAN
THIS BOOK IS DEDICATED
WITH WARM AND DEEP REGARDS

AVALON,
JULY 10TH, 1907

CONTENTS

DAYS OFF

DAYS OFF

"A DAY OFF," said my Uncle Peter, settling down in his chair before the open wood-fire, with that air of complacent obstinacy which spreads over him when he is about to confess and expound his philosophy of life,—"a day off is a day that a man takes to himself."

"You mean a day of luxurious solitude," I said, "a stolen sweet of time, which he carries away into some hidden corner to enjoy alone,— a little-Jack-Horner kind of a day?"

"Not at all," said my Uncle Peter; "solitude is a thing which a man hardly ever enjoys by himself. He may practise it from a sense of duty. Or he may take refuge in it from other things that are less tolerable. But nine times out of ten he will find that he can't get a really good day to himself unless he shares it with some one else; if he takes it alone, it will be a heavy day, a chain-and-ball day,—anything but a day off."

"Just what do you mean, then?" I asked, knowing that nothing would please him better than the chance to discover his own meaning

3

against a little background of apparent misunderstanding and opposition.

"I mean," said my Uncle Peter, in that deliberate manner which lends a flavour of deep wisdom to the most obvious remarks, "I mean that every man owes it to himself to have some days in his life when he escapes from bondage, gets away from routine, and does something which seems to have no purpose in the world, just because he wants to do it."

"Plays truant," I interjected.

"Yes, if you like to put it in that objectionable way," he answered; "but I should rather compare it to bringing flowers into the schoolroom, or keeping white mice in your desk, or inventing a new game for the recess. You see we are all scholars, boarding scholars, in the House of Life, from the moment when birth matriculates us to the moment when death graduates us. We never really leave the big school, no matter what we do. But my point is this: the lessons that we learn when we do not know that we are studying are often the pleasantest, and not always the least important. There is a benefit as well as a joy in finding out that you can lay down your task for a proper while without being disloyal to your duty. Play-time is a part of school-time, not a break in it. You remember what Aristotle says: '*ascholoumetha gar hina scholazomen.*'"

"My dear uncle," said I, "there is nothing out of the common in your remarks, except of course your extraordinary habit of decorating them with a Greek quotation, like an ancient coin set as a scarf-pin and stuck carelessly into a modern neck-tie. But apart from this eccentricity, everybody admits the propriety of what you have been saying. Why, all the expensive, up-to-date schools are arranged on your principle: play-hours, exercise-hours, silent-hours, social-hours, all marked in the schedule: scholars compelled and carefully guided to amuse themselves at set times and in approved fashions: athletics, dramatics, school-politics and social ethics, all organized and co-ordinated. What you flatter yourself by putting forward as an amiable heresy has become a commonplace of orthodoxy, and your liberal theory of education and life is now one of the marks of fashionable conservatism."

My Uncle Peter's face assumed the beatific expression of a man who knows that he has been completely and inexcusably misunderstood, and is therefore justified in taking as much time as he wants to make the subtlety and superiority of his ideas perfectly clear and to show how dense you have been in failing to apprehend them.

"My dear boy," said he, "it is very singular that you should miss my point so entirely. All these things that you have been saying about your modern schools illustrate precisely the opposite view from mine. They are signs of that idolatry of organization, of system, of the time-table and the schedule, which is making our modern life so tedious and exhausting. Those unfortunate school-boys and school-girls who have their amusements planned out for them and cultivate their social instincts according to rule, never know the joy of a real day off, unless they do as I say, and take it to themselves. The right kind of a school will leave room and liberty for them to do this. It will be a miniature of what life is for all of us,— a place where law reigns and independence is rewarded,—a stream of work and duty diversified by islands of freedom and repose,—a pilgrimage in which it is permitted to follow a side-path, a mountain trail, a footway through the meadow, provided the end of the journey is not forgotten and the day's march brings one a little nearer to that end."

"But will it do that," I asked, "unless one is

careful to follow the straight line of the highway and march as fast as one can?"

"That depends," said my Uncle Peter, nodding his head gravely, "upon what you consider the end of the journey. If it is something entirely outside of yourself, a certain stint of work which you were created to perform; or if it is something altogether beyond yourself, a certain place or office at which you are aiming to arrive; then, of course, you must stick to the highway and hurry along.

"But suppose that the real end of your journey is something of which you yourself are a part. Suppose it is not merely to get to a certain place, but to get there in a certain condition, with the light of a sane joy in your eyes and the peace of a grateful content in your heart. Suppose it is not merely to do a certain piece of work, but to do it in a certain spirit, cheerfully and bravely and modestly, without overrating its importance or overlooking its necessity. Then, I fancy, you may find that the winding foot-path among the hills often helps you on your way as much as the high road, the day off among the islands of repose gives you a steadier hand and a braver heart to make your voyage along the stream of duty."

"You may skip the moralizing, if you please,

Uncle Peter," said I, "and concentrate your mind upon giving me a reasonable account of the peculiar happiness of what you call a day off."

"Nothing could be simpler," he answered. "It is the joy of getting out of the harness that makes a horse fling up his heels, and gallop around the field, and roll over and over in the grass, when he is turned loose in the pasture. It is the impulse of pure play that makes a little bunch of wild ducks chase one another round and round on the water, and follow their leader in circles and figures of eight; there is no possible use in it, but it gratifies their instinct of freedom and makes them feel that they are not mere animal automata, whatever some natural history men may say to the contrary. It is the sense of release that a man experiences when he unbuckles the straps of his knapsack, and lays it down under a tree, and says 'You stay there till I come back for you! I'm going to rest myself by climbing this hill, just because it is not on the road-map, and because there is nothing at the top of it except the view.'

"It is this feeling of escape," he continued, in the tone of a man who has shaken off the harness of polite conversation and let himself go

8

for a gallop around the field of monologue, "it is just this exhilarating sense of liberation that is lacking in most of our social amusements and recreations. They are dictated by fashion and directed by routine. Men get into the so-called 'round of pleasure,' and they are driven into a trot to keep up with it, just as if it were a treadmill. The only difference is that the pleasure-mill grinds no corn. Harry Bellairs was complaining to me, the other day, that after an exhausting season of cotillons in New York, he had been running his motor-car through immense fatigues in France and Italy, and had returned barely in time to do his duty by his salmon-river in Canada, work his new boat through the annual cruise of the yacht club, finish up a round of house-parties at Bar Harbor and Lenox, and get ready for the partridge-shooting in England with his friend the Duke of Bangham,—it was a dog's life, he said, and he had no time to himself at all. I rather pitied him; he looked so frayed. It seems to me that the best way for a man or a woman of pleasure to get a day off would be to do a little honest work.

"You see it is the change that makes the charm of a day off. The real joy of leisure is known only to the people who have contracted

9

the habit of work without becoming enslaved to the vice of overwork.

"A hobby is the best thing in the world for a man with a serious vocation. It keeps him from getting muscle-bound in his own task. It helps to save him from the mistake of supposing that it is his little tick-tack that keeps the universe a-going. It leads him out, on days off, away from his own garden corner into curious and interesting regions of this wide and various earth, of which, after all, he is a citizen.

"Do you happen to know the Reverend Doctor McHook? He is a learned preacher, a devoted churchman, a faithful minister; and in addition to this he has an extra-parochial affection for ants and spiders. He can spend a happy day in watching the busy affairs of a formicary, and to observe the progress of a bit of spider-web architecture gives him a peculiar joy. There are some severe and sour-complexioned theologians who would call this devotion to objects so far outside of his parish an illicit passion. But to me it seems a blessing conferred by heavenly wisdom upon a good man, and I doubt not he escapes from many an insoluble theological puzzle, and perhaps from many an unprofitable religious wrangle, to find refreshment and invigoration in the society of his many-legged friends."

10

DAYS OFF

"You are moralizing again, Uncle Peter," I objected; "or at least you are getting ready to do so. Stop it; and give me a working definition of the difference between a hobby and a fad."

"Let me give you an anecdote," said he, "instead of a definition. There was a friend of mine who went to visit a famous asylum for the insane. Among the patients who were amusing themselves in the great hall, he saw an old gentleman with a long white beard, who was sitting astride of a chair, spurring its legs with his heels, holding both ends of his handkerchief which he had knotted around the back, and crying 'Get up, get up! G'long boy, steady!' with the utmost animation. 'You seem to be having a fine ride, sir,' said my friend. 'Capital,' said the old gentleman, 'this is a first-rate mount that I am riding.' 'Permit me to inquire,' asked my friend, 'whether it is a fad or a hobby?' 'Why, certainly!' replied the old gentleman, with a quizzical look. 'It is a hobby, you see, for I can get off whenever I have a mind to.' And with that he dismounted and walked into the garden.

"It is just this liberty of getting off that marks the superiority of a hobby to a fad. The game that you feel obliged to play every day at the same hour ceases to amuse you as soon as you realize that it is a diurnal duty. Regular

11

exercise is good for the muscles, but there must be a bit of pure fun mixed with the sport that is to refresh your heart.

"A tour in Europe, carefully mapped out with an elaborate itinerary and a carefully connected time-table, may be full of instruction, but it often becomes a tax upon the spirit and a weariness to the flesh. Compulsory castles and mandatory museums and required ruins pall upon you, as you hurry from one to another, vaguely agitated by the fear that you may miss something that is marked with a star in the guidebook, and so be compelled to confess to your neighbour at the *table-d'hote* that you have failed to see what he promptly and joyfully assures you is 'the best thing in the whole trip.' Delicate and sensitive people have been killed by taking a vacation in that way.

"I remember meeting, several years ago, a party of personally conducted tourists in Venice, at the hour which their itinerary consecrated to the enjoyment of the fine arts in the gallery of the Academy. Their personal conductor led them into one of the great rooms, and they gathered close around him, with an air of determination on their tired faces, listening to his brief, dry patter about the famous pictures that the room contained. He stood in

12

the centre of the room holding his watch in his
hand while they dispersed themselves around
the walls, looking for the paintings which they
ought to see, like chickens searching for scattered grains of corn. At the expiration of five
minutes he clapped his hands sharply; his flock
scurried back to him; and they moved on to
'do' the next room.

"I suppose that is one way of seeing Venice:
but I would much rather sit at a little table on
the *Riva degli Schiavoni*, with a plate of bread
and cheese and a *mezzo* of Chianti before me,
watching the motley crowd in the street and the
many-coloured sails in the harbour; or spend a
lazy afternoon in a gondola, floating through
watery alley-ways that lead nowhere, and under
the façades of beautiful palaces whose names I
did not even care to know. Of course I should
like to see a fine picture or a noble church, now
and then; but only one at a time, if you please;
and that one I should wish to look at as long
as it said anything to me, and to revisit as often
as it called me."

"That is because you have no idea of the
educational uses of a vacation, Uncle Peter,"
said I. "You are an unsystematic person, an
incorrigible idler."

"I am," he answered, without a sign of peni-

13

tence, "that is precisely what I am,—in my days off. Otherwise I should not get the good of them. Even a hobby, on such days, is to be used chiefly for its lateral advantages,—the open doors of the side-shows to which it brings you, the unexpected opportunities of dismounting and tying your hobby to a tree, while you follow the trail of something strange and attractive, as Moses did when he turned aside from his shepherding on Mount Horeb and climbed up among the rocks to see the burning bush.

"The value of a favourite pursuit lies not only in its calculated results but also in its by-products. You may become a collector of almost anything in the world,—orchids, postage-stamps, flint arrowheads, cook-books, varieties of the game of cat's cradle,—and if you chase your trifle in the right spirit it will lead you into pleasant surprises and bring you acquainted with delightful or amusing people. You remember when you went with Professor Rinascimento on a Della Robbia hunt among the hill towns of Italy, and how you came by accident into that deep green valley where there are more nightingales with sweeter voices than anywhere else on earth? Your best *trouvaille* on that expedition was hidden in those undreamed-of nights of moonlight and music. And it was when you were chasing first editions of Tennyson, was it not, that you discovered your little head of a marble faun, which you vow is by Donatello, or one of his pupils? And what was it that you told me about the rare friend you found when you took a couple of days off in an ancient French town, on a flying journey from Rome to London? Believe me, dear boy, all that we win by effort and intention is sometimes overtopped by a gift that is conferred upon us out of a secret and mysterious generosity. Wordsworth was right:

> "'Think you, 'mid all this mighty sum
>   Of things forever speaking,
> That nothing of itself will come,
>   But we must still be seeking?'"

"You talk," said I, "as if you thought it was a man's duty to be happy."

"I do," he answered firmly, "that is precisely and definitely what I think. It is not his chief duty, nor his only duty, nor his duty all the time. But the normal man is not intended to go through this world without learning what happiness means. If he does so he misses something that he needs to complete his nature and perfect his experience. 'Tis a poor, frail plant that can not endure the wind and the rain and the winter's cold. But is it a good plant that will not respond to the quickening touch of spring and send out its sweet odours in the embracing warmth of the summer night? Suppose that you had made a house for a child, and given him a corner of the garden to keep, and set him lessons and tasks, and provided him with teachers and masters. Would you be satisfied with that child, however diligent and obedient, if you found that he was never happy, never enjoyed a holiday, never said to himself and to you, 'What a good place this is, and how glad I am to live here'?"

"Probably not," I answered, "but that is because I should be selfish enough to find a pleasure of my own in his happiness. I should like to take a day off with him, now and then, and his gladness would increase my enjoyment. There is no morality in that. It is simply natural. We are all made that way."

"Well," said my Uncle Peter, "if we are made that way we must take it into account in our philosophy of life. The fact that it is natural is not a sufficient reason for concluding that it is bad. There is an old and wonderful book which describes the creation of the world in poetic language; and when I read that description it makes me feel sure that something like this was purposely woven into the very

16

web of life. After the six mystical days of making things and putting things in order, says this beautiful old book, the Person who had been doing it all took a day to Himself, in which He 'rested from all the things that He had created and made,' and looked at them, and saw how good they were. His work was not ended, of course, for it has been going on ever since, and will go on for ages of ages. But in the midst of it all it seemed right to Him to take a divine day off. And His example is commended to us for imitation because we are made in His likeness and have the same desire to enjoy as well as to create.

"Do you remember what the Wisest of all Masters said to his disciples when they were outworn by the weight of their work and the pressure of the crowd upon them? 'Come ye yourselves apart into a lonely place, and rest awhile.' He would never have bidden them do that, unless it had been a part of their duty to get away from their task for a little. He knew what was in man, more deeply than any one else had ever known; and so he invited his friends out among the green hills and beside the quiet waters of Galilee to the strengthening repose and the restoring joy which are only to be found in real days off."

My Uncle Peter's voice had grown deep and

gentle while he was saying these things. He sat looking far away into the rosy heart of the fire, where the bright blaze had burned itself out, and the delicate flamelets of blue and violet were playing over the glowing, crumbling logs. It seemed as if he had forgotten where we were, and gone a-wandering into some distant region of memories and dreams. I almost doubted whether to call him back; the silence was so full of comfortable and friendly intercourse.

"Well," said I, after a while, "you are an incorrigible moralist, but certainly a most unconventional one. The orthodox would never accept your philosophy. They would call you a hedonist, or something equally dreadful."

"Let them," he said, placidly.

"But tell me": I asked, "you and I have many pleasant and grateful memories, little pictures and stories, which seem like chapters in the history of this doubtful idea of yours: suppose that I should write some of them down, purely in a descriptive and narrative way, without committing myself to any opinion as to their morality; and suppose that a few of your opinions and prejudices, briefly expressed, were interspersed in the form of chapters to be skipped: would a book like that symbolize and illustrate the true inwardness of the day off? How would it do to make such a book?"

18

"It would do," he answered, "provided you wanted to do it, and provided you did not try to prove anything, or convince anybody, or convey any profitable instruction."

"But would any one read it?" I asked. "What do you think?"

"I think," said he, stretching his arms over his head as he rose and turned towards his den to plunge into a long evening's work, "I reckon, and calculate, and fancy, and guess that a few people, a very few, might browse through such a book in their days off."

A HOLIDAY IN A VACATION

A HOLIDAY IN A VACATION

IT was really a good little summer resort where the boy and I were pegging away at our vacation. There were the mountains conveniently arranged, with pleasant trails running up all of them, carefully marked with rustic but legible guide-posts; and there was the sea comfortably besprinkled with islands, among which one might sail around and about, day after day, not to go anywhere, but just to enjoy the motion and the views; and there were cod and haddock swimming over the outer ledges in deep water, waiting to be fed with clams at any time, and on fortunate days ridiculously accommodating in letting themselves be pulled up at the end of a long, thick string with a pound of lead and two hooks tied to it. There were plenty of places considered proper for picnics, like Jordan's Pond, and Great Cranberry Island, and the Russian Tea-house, and the Log Cabin Tea-house, where you would be sure to meet other people who also were bent on picnicking; and there were hotels and summer cottages, of various degrees of elaboration, filled with agreeable and talkable folk, most of whom were connected by occupation or marriage with the rival colleges and universities, so that their ambitions for the simple life had an academic thoroughness and regularity. There were dinner parties, and tea parties, and garden parties, and sea parties, and luncheon parties, masculine and feminine, and a horse-show at Bar Harbor, and a gymkhana at North East, and dances at all the Harbors, where Minerva met Terpsichore on a friendly footing while Socrates sat out on the veranda with Midas discussing the great automobile question over their cigars.

It was all vastly entertaining and well-ordered, and you would think that any person with a properly constituted mind ought to be able to peg through a vacation in such a place without wavering. But when the boy confessed to me that he felt the need of a few "days off" in the big woods to keep him up to his duty, I saw at once that the money spent upon his education had not been wasted; for here, without effort, he announced a great psychological fact—*that no vacation is perfect without a holiday in it.* So we packed our camping-kit, made our peace with the family, tied our engagements together and cut the string below the knot, and set out to find freedom and a little fishing in the region around Lake Nicatöus.

The south-east corner of the State of Maine is a happy remnant of the ancient wilderness. The railroads will carry you around it in a day, if you wish to go that way, making a big oval of two or three hundred miles along the sea and by the banks of the Penobscot, the Mattawam-keag, and the St. Croix. But if you wisely wish to go through the oval you must ride, or go afoot, or take to your canoe; probably you will have to try all three methods of locomotion, for the country is a mixed quantity. It re-minds me of what I once heard in Stockholm: that the Creator, when the making of the rest of the world was done, had a lot of fragments of land and water, forests and meadows, moun-tains and valleys, lakes and moors, left over; and these He threw together to make the south-ern part of Sweden. I like that kind of a promiscuous country. The spice of life grows there.

When we had escaped from the railroad at Enfield on the Penobscot, we slept a short night in a room over a country store, and took wagon the next morning for a twenty-five mile drive. At the somnolent little village of Burlington we found our guides waiting for us. They were sitting on the green at the cross-roads, with their paddles and axes and bundles beside them. I knew at a glance that they were ready and all right: Sam Dam, an old experienced, seasoned guide, and Harry, a good-looking young woodsman who had worked in lumber camps and on "the drive," but had never been "guidin'" before. He was little the worse for that, for he belonged to the type of Maine man who has the faculty of learning things by doing them.

As we rattled along the road the farms grew poorer and sparser, until at last we came into the woods, crossed the rocky Passadumkeag River, and so over a succession of horseback hills to the landing-place on Nicatöus Stream, where the canoes were hidden in the bushes. Now load up with the bundles and boxes, the tent, the blanket-roll, the clothes-bag, the provisions—all the stuff that is known as "duffel" in New York, and *"butins"* in French Canada, and *"wangan"* in Maine—stow it all away judiciously so that the two light craft will be well balanced; and then push off, paddles, and let us taste the joy of a new stream! New to the boy and me, you understand; but to the guides it was old and familiar, a link in a much-travelled route. The amber water rippled merrily over the rocky bars where the river was low, and in the still reaches it spread out broad and smooth, covered with white lilies and fringed with tall grasses. All along the pleasant way Sam entertained us with memories of the stream.

"Ye see that grassy p'int, jest ahead of us? Three weeks ago I was comin' down for the mail, and there was three deer a-stannin' on that p'int, a buck and a doe and a fawn. And——"

"Up in them alders there's a little spring brook comes in. Good fishin' there in high water. But now? Well——"

"Jest beyond that bunch o' rocks last fall there was three fellers comin' down in a canoe, and a big bear come out and started 'cross river. The gun was in the case in the bottom of the canoe, and one o' the fellers had a pistol, and so——"

Beyond a doubt it was so, always has been so, and always will be so—just so, on every river travelled by canoes, until the end of time. The sportsman travels through a happy interval between memories of failure and expectation of success. But the river and the wind in the trees sing to him by the way, and there are wild flowers along the banks, and every turn in the stream makes a new picture of beauty. Thus we came leisurely and peacefully to the place where the river issued from the lake; and here we must fish awhile, for it was reported that the landlocked salmon lay in the narrow channel just above the dam.

Sure enough, no sooner had the fly crossed the current than there was a rise; and at the second cast a pretty salmon of two and a half pounds was hooked, played, and landed. Three more were taken, of which the boy got two— and his were the biggest. Fish know nothing of the respect due to age. They leaped well, those little salmon, flashing clean out of the water again and again with silvery gleams. But on the whole they did not play as strongly nor as long as their brethren (called *ouananiche*,) in the wild rapids where the Upper Saguenay breaks from Lake St. John. The same fish are always more lively, powerful, and enduring when they live in swift water, battling with the current, than when they vegetate in the quiet depths of a lake. But if a salmon must live in a luxurious home of that kind, Nicatöus is a good one, for the water is clear, the shores are clean, the islands plenty, and the bays deep and winding.

At the club-house, six miles up the lake, where we arrived at candle-lighting, we found such kindly welcome and good company that we tarried for three days in that woodland Capua, discussing the further course of our expedition. Everybody was willing to lend us aid and comfort. The sociable hermit who had summered for the last twenty years in his tiny cabin on the point gave us friendly counsel and excellent large blueberries. The matron provided us with daily bags of most delicate tea, a precaution against the native habit of "squatting" the leaves—that is, boiling and squeezing them to extract the tannin. The little lady called Katharyne (a fearless forest-maid who roamed the woods in leathern jacket and short blue skirt, followed by an enormous and admiring guide, and caught big fish everywhere) offered to lend us anything in her outfit, from a pack-basket to a darning-needle. It was cheerful to meet with such general encouragement in our small adventure. But the trouble was to decide which way to go.

Nicatöus lies near the top of a watershed about a thousand feet high. From the region round about it at least seven canoeable rivers descend to civilization. The Narraguagus and the Union on the south, the Passadumkeag on the west, the Sisladobsis and the St. Croix on the north, and the two branches of the Machias or Kowahshiscook on the east; to say nothing of the Westogus and the Hackmatack and the Mopang. Here were names to stir the fancy and paralyze the tongue. What a joy to follow one of these streams clear through its course and come out of the woods in our own craft—from Nicatöus to the sea!

It was perhaps something in the name, some wild generosity of alphabetical expenditure, that led us to the choice of the Kowahshiscook, or west branch of the Machias River. Or perhaps it was because neither of our guides had been down that stream, and so the whole voyage would be an exploration, with everybody on the same level of experience. An easy day's journey across the lake, and up Comb's Brook, where the trout were abundant, and by a two-mile carry into Horseshoe Lake, and then over a narrow hardwood ridge, brought us to Green Lake, where we camped for the night in a new log shanty.

Here we were at the topmost source—*fons et origo*—of our chosen river. This single spring, crystal-clear and ice-cold, gushing out of the hillside in a forest of spruce and yellow birch and sugar maple, gave us the clue that we must follow for a week through the wilderness.

But how changed was that transparent rivulet after it entered the lake. There the water was pale green, translucent but semi-opaque, for at a depth of two or three feet the bottom was hardly visible. The lake was filled, I believe, with some minute aquatic growth which in the course of a thousand years or so would transform it into a meadow. But meantime the mystical water was inhabited, especially around the mouth of the spring, by huge trout to whom tradition ascribed a singular and provoking disposition. They would take the bait, when the fancy moved them: but the fly they would always refuse, ignoring it with calm disdain, or slapping at it with their tails and shoving it out of their way as they played on the surface in the summer evenings. This was the mysterious reputation of the trout of Green Lake, handed down from generation to generation of anglers; and this spell we had come to break, by finding the particular fly that would be irresistible to those secret epicures and the psychological moment of the day when they could no longer resist temptation. We tried all the flies in our books; at sunset, in the twilight, by the light of the stars and the rising moon, at dawn and at sunrise. Not one trout did we capture with the fly in Green Lake. Nor could we solve the mystery of those reluctant fish. The boy made a scientific suggestion that they got plenty of food from the cloudy water, which served them as a kind of soup. My guess was that their sight was impaired so that they could not see the fly. But Sam said it was "jest pure cussedness." Many things in the world happen from that cause, and as a rule it is best not to fret over them.

The trail from Green Lake to Campbell Lake was easily found; it followed down the outlet about a mile. But it had been little used for many years and the undergrowth had almost obliterated it. Rain had been falling all the morning and the bushes were wetter than water. On such a carry travel is slow. We had three trips to make each way before we could get the stuff and the canoes over. Then a short voyage across the lake, and another mile of the same sort of portage, after which we came out with the last load, an hour before sundown, on the shore of the Big Sabeo. This lake was quite different from the others; wide and open, with smooth sand-beaches all around it. The little hills which encircled it had been burned over years ago; and the blueberry pickers had renewed the fire from year to year. The landscape was light green and yellow, beneath a low, cloudy sky; no forest in sight, except one big, black island far across the water.

The place where we came out was not attractive; but nothing is more foolish than to go on looking for a pretty camp-ground after daylight has begun to wane. When the sun comes within the width of two paddle-blades of the horizon, if you are wise you will take the first bit of level ground within reach of wood and water, and make haste to get the camp in order before dark. So we pitched our blue tent on the beach, with a screen of bushes at the back to shelter us from the wind; broke a double quantity of fir branches for our bed, to save us from the midnight misery of sand in the blankets; cut a generous supply of firewood from a dead pine-tree which stood conveniently at hand; and settled down in comfort for the night.

What could have been better than our supper, cooked in the open air and eaten by firelight! True, we had no plates—they had been forgotten—but we never mourned for them. We made a shift to get along with the tops of some emptied tin cans and the cover of a kettle; and from these rude platters, (quite as serviceable as the porcelain of Limoges or Sèvres) we consumed our toast, and our boiled potatoes with butter, and our trout prudently brought from Horseshoe Lake, and, best of all, our bacon.

Do you remember what Charles Lamb says

about roast pig? How he falls into an ecstasy
of laudation, spelling the very name with small
capitals, as if the lower case were too mean for
such a delicacy, and breaking away from the
cheap encomiums of the vulgar tongue to hail
it in sonorous Latin as *princeps obsoniorum!*
There is some truth in his compliments, no
doubt; but they are wasteful, excessive, impru-
dent. For if all this praise is to be lavished on
plain, fresh, immature, roast pig, what adjec-
tives shall we find to do justice to that riper,
richer, more subtle and sustaining viand, broiled
bacon? On roast pig a man can not work;
often he can not sleep, if he have partaken of it
immoderately. But bacon "brings to its sweetness no satiety." It strengthens the arm while
it satisfies the palate. Crisp, juicy, savory;
delicately salt as the breeze that blows from the
sea; faintly pungent as the blue smoke of in-
cense wafted from a clean wood-fire; aromatic,
appetizing, nourishing, a stimulant to the hunger which it appeases, 'tis the matured bloom
and consummation of the mild little pig, spared
by foresight for a nobler fate than juvenile
roasting, and brought by art and man's device
to a perfection surpassing nature. All the
problems of woodland cookery are best solved
by the baconian method. And when we say of

one escaping great disaster that he has "saved
his bacon," we say that the physical basis and
the quintessential comfort of his life are still
untouched and secure.

Steadily fell the rain all that night, plentiful,
persistent, drumming on the tightened canvas
over our heads, waking us now and then to
pleasant thoughts of a rising stream and good
water for the morrow. Breaking clouds rolled
before the sunrise, and the lake was all a-glitter
when we pushed away in dancing canoes to find
the outlet. This is one of the problems in
which the voyager learns to know something of
the infinite reserve, the humorous subtlety, the
hide-and-seek quality in nature. Where is it—
that mysterious outlet? Behind yonder long
point? Nothing here but a narrow arm of the
lake. At the end of this deep bay? Nothing
here but a little brook flowing in. At the back
of the island? Nothing here but a landlocked
lagoon. Must we make the circuit of the
whole shore before we find the way out? Stop
a moment. What are those two taller clumps
of bushes on the edge of this broad curving
meadow—down there in the corner, do you
see? Turn back, go close to the shore, swing
around the nearer clump, and here we are in
the smooth amber stream, slipping silently, fur-

tively, down through the meadow, as if it would steal away for a merry jest and leave us going round and round the lake till nightfall.

Easily and swiftly the canoes slide along with the little river, winding and doubling through the wide, wild field, travelling three miles to gain one. The rushes nod and glisten around us; the bending reeds whisper as we push between them, cutting across a point. Follow the stream; we know not its course, but we know that if we go with it, though it be a wayward and tricksy guide, it will bring us out— but not too soon, we hope!

Here is a lumberman's dam, broad-based, solid, and ugly, a work of infinite labour, standing lonely, deserted, here in the heart of the wilderness. Now we must carry across it. But it shall help while it hinders us. Pry up the creaking sluice-gates, sending a fresh head of water down the channel along with us, lifting us over the shallows, driving us on through the rocky places, buoyant, alert, and rejoicing, till we come again to a level meadow, and the long, calm, indolent reaches of river.

Look on the right there, under the bushes. There is a cold, still brook, slipping into the lazy river; and there we must try the truth of the tales we have heard of the plentiful trout of Machias. Let the flies fall light by the mouth of the brook, caressing, inviting. Nothing there? Then push the canoe through the interlaced alders, quietly, slowly up the narrow stream, till a wider pool lies open before you. Now let the rod swing high in the air, lifting the line above the bushes, dropping the flies as far away as you can on the dark-brown water. See how quickly the answer comes, in two swift golden flashes out of the depths of the sleeping pool. This is a pretty brace of trout, from thirty to forty ounces of thoroughbred fighting pluck, and the spirit that will not surrender. If they only knew that their strength would be doubled by acting together, they soon would tangle your line in the roots or break your rod in the alders. But all the time they are fighting against each other, making it easy to bring them up to the net and land them—a pair of beauties, evenly matched in weight and in splendour, gleaming with rich iridescent hues of orange and green and peacock-blue and crimson. A few feet beyond you find another, a smaller fish, and then one a little larger; and so you go on up the stream, threading the boat through the alders, with patience and infinite caution, carefully casting your flies when the stream opens out to invite them, till you have rounded your dozen of trout and are wisely contented. Then you go backward down the brook—too narrow for turning—and join the other canoe that waits, floating leisurely on with the river.

There is a change now in the character of the stream. The low hills that have been standing far away, come close together from either side, as if they meant to bar any further passage; and the dreamy river wakes up to wrestle its way down the narrow valley. There are no long, sleepy reaches, no wide, easy curves, now; but sharp, quick turns from one rocky ledge to another; and enormous stones piled and scattered along the river-bed; and sudden descents from level to level as if by the broad steps of a ruined, winding stairway. The water pushes, and rushes, and roars, and foams, and frets— no, it does not fret, after all, for there is always something joyous and exultant in its voice, a note of the *gaudia certaminis* by which the struggle of life is animated, a note of confident strength, sure that it can find or make a way, through all obstacles, to its goal. This is what I feel in a river, especially a little river flowing through a rough, steep country. This is what makes me love it. It seems to be thoroughly alive, and glad to be alive, and determined to go on, and certain that it will win through.

A HOLIDAY IN A VACATION

Our canoes go with the river, but no longer
easily or lazily. Every step of the way must
be carefully chosen; now close to the steep bank
where the bushes hang over; now in mid-stream
among the huge pointed rocks; now by the lowest point of a broad sunken ledge where the
water sweeps smoothly over to drop into the
next pool. The boy and I, using the bow paddles, are in the front of the adventure, guessing
at the best channel, pushing aside suddenly to
avoid treacherous stones hidden with dark moss,
dashing swiftly down the long dancing rapids,
with the shouting of the waves in our ears and
the sprinkle of the foam in our faces.

From side to side of the wild avenue through
the forest we turn and dart, zigzagging among
the rocks. Thick woods shut us in on either
hand, pines and hemlocks and firs and spruces,
beeches and maples and yellow-birches, alders
with their brown seed-cones, and mountain-
ashes with their scarlet berries. All four of us
know the way; there can be no doubt about
that, for down the river is the only road out.
But none of us knows the path; for this is a
new stream, you remember, and between us
and our journey's end there lie a thousand possible difficulties, accidents, and escapes.

The boy had one of them. His canoe struck
on a ledge, in passing over a little fall, swung

39

around sidewise to the current, and half filled with water; he and Harry had to leap out into the stream waist-deep. Sam and I made merry at their plight. But Nemesis was waiting for me a few miles below.

All the pools were full of fine trout. While the men were cooking lunch in a grove of balsams I waded down-stream to get another brace of fish. Stepping carefully among the rocks, I stood about thigh-deep in my rubber boots and cast across the pool. But the best bit of water was a little beyond my reach. A step further! There is a yellow bit of gravel that will give a good footing. Intent upon the flight of my flies, I took the step without care. But the yellow patch under the brown water was not gravel; it was the face of a rock polished smoother than glass. Gently, slowly, irresistibly, and with deep indignation I subsided backward into the cold pool. The rubber boots filled with water and the immersion was complete. Then I stood up and got the trout. When I returned to the camp-fire, the others laughed at me uproariously, and the boy said: "Why did you go in swimming with your clothes on? Were you expecting a party of ladies to come down the stream?"

Our tenting-places were new every night and

forsaken every morning. Each of them had a
charm of its own. One was under a great yel-
low-birch tree, close to the bank of the river.
Another was on top of a bare ridge in the middle of a vast blueberry patch, where the luscious
fruit, cool and fresh with the morning dew,
spread an immense breakfast-table to tempt us.
The most beautiful of all was at the edge of a
fir-wood, with a huge rock, covered with moss
and lichen, sloping down before us in a broad,
open descent of thirty feet to the foaming
stream. The full moon climbed into the sky
as we sat around our camp-fire, and showed her
face above the dark, pointed tree-tops. The
winding vale was flooded with silver radiance
that rested on river and rock and tree-trunk
and multitudinous leafage like an enchantment
of tranquillity. The curling currents and the
floating foam, up and down the stream, were
glistening and sparkling, ever moving, yet never
losing their position. The shouting of the water
melted to music, in which a thousand strange
and secret voices, near and far away, blending
and alternating from rapid to rapid and fall to
fall, seemed like hidden choirs, answering one
another from place to place. The sense of
struggle, of pressure and resistance, of perpetual
change, was gone; and in its stead there was a

feeling of infinite quietude, of perfect balance and repose, of deep accord and amity between the watching heavens and the waiting earth, in which the conflicts of existence seemed very distant and of little meaning, and the peace of nature prophesied

" That one, far-off divine event
Towards which the whole creation moves."

Thus for six days and nights we kept company with our little river, following its guidance and enjoying all its changing moods. Sometimes it led us through a smooth country, across natural meadows, alder-fringed, where the bed of the stream was of amber sand and polished gravel, and the water rippled gently over the shallow bars, and there were deep holes underneath the hanging bushes, where the trout hid from the heat of the noon sun. Sometimes it had carved a way for itself over huge beds of solid rock, where, if the slope was gentle, we could dart arrow-like along the channel from pool to pool; but if the descent was steep and broken, we must get out of the canoes and let them down with ropes. Sometimes the course ran for miles through evergreen forests, where the fragrance of the fir-trees filled the air; and again we came out into the open regions where thousands of acres of wild blueberries were spread around us.

I call them wild because no man's hand has planted them. Yet they are cultivated after a fashion. Every two or three years a district of these hills is set on fire, and in the burned land, the next spring, the berry-bushes come up innumerable. The following fall they are loaded so heavily with blueberries that the harvest is gathered with rakes, each of which has a cup underneath it into which the berries fall as the rake goes through the bushes. The land is owned by two or three large proprietors, who employ men and women to gather the crop, paying them a few cents a bushel for picking. Sometimes the proprietor leases his land to a factor, who pays a royalty on every bushel turned in at the factory in some village on the railroad or by the seashore, where the berries are canned or dried.

One day we came upon a camp of these berry-pickers by the river-side. Our first notice of their proximity was the sight of a raft with an arm-chair tied in the centre of it, stranded upon the rocks in a long, fierce rapid. Imagine how this looked to us after we had been five days in the wilderness! An arm-chair sitting up sedately in the middle of the rapids! What did it mean? Perhaps some vagrant artist had been exploring the river, and had fixed his seat there in order to paint a picture. Perhaps some lazy fisherman had found a good pool amid those boiling waters, and had arranged to take his ease while he whipped that fishy place with his flies. The mystery was solved when we rounded the next point; for there we found the berry-pickers taking their nooning in a cluster of little slab-shanties. They were friendly folks, men, women, and children, but they knew nothing about the river; had never been up farther than the place where the boys had left their raft in the high water a week ago; had never been down at all; could not tell how many falls there were below, nor whether the mouth was five or fifty miles away. They had come in by the road, which crossed the river at this point, and by the road they would go back when the berries were picked. They wanted to know whether we were prospecting for lumber or thinking of going into the berry business. We tried to explain the nature of our expedition to them, but I reckon we failed.

These were the only people that we really met on our journey, though we saw a few others far off on some bare hill. We did not encounter a single boat or canoe on the river. But we saw the deer come down to the shore, and stand shoulder-deep among the golden-rod and purple asters. We saw the ruffed grouse whir through the thickets and the wild ducks skitter down the stream ahead of us. We saw the warblers and the cedar-birds gathering in flocks for their southward flight, the muskrats making their houses ready for the winter, and the porcupines dumbly meditating and masticating among the branches of the young poplar-trees. We also had a delightful interview with a wildcat, and almost a thrilling adventure with a bear.

The boy and I had started out from camp for an hour of evening fishing. He went down the stream some distance ahead of me, as I supposed, (though, as I afterward found, he had made a little détour and turned back). I was making my way painfully through a spruce thicket when I heard a loud crash and crackling of dead branches. "Hallo!" I cried; "have you fallen down? Are you hurt?" No answer. "Hallo, Teddy!" I shouted again; "what's the matter?" At this ominous name there was a tremendous crash, and then dead silence.

I dropped my rod and pushed as rapidly as possible in the direction from which the sound had come. There I found a circle about fifty feet in diameter torn and trampled as if a circus had been there. The ground was trodden bare. Trees three and four inches thick were broken off. The bark of the larger trees was stripped away. The place was a ruin. A few paces away, among the bushes, there was a bear trap with some claws in it, and an iron chain attached to the middle of a clog about four feet long. The log hovel in which the trap had been set we found later a little way back on an old wood road. Evidently a bear had been caught there, perhaps two or three days before we came. He had dragged the trap and the chained clog down into the thicket. There he had stayed, tearing up things generally in his efforts to escape from his encumbrance, and resting quietly in the intervals of his fury. My approach had startled him and he had made the first crash. Then he lay low and listened. My second inconsiderate shout of "Hallo, *Teddy !*" had put such an enormous fear into him that he dashed through the trees, caught the foolishly chained clog across two of them, and, tearing himself loose, escaped with the loss of a couple of toes. Thus ended our almost adventure with a bear. How glad the old fellow must have been !

The moral is this: If you want a bear, you should set your trap with the clog chained at one end, not around the middle: then it will trail through the woods and not break loose. But the best way is not to want a bear.

Our last camp was just at the head of Holmes's Fall, a splendid ravine down which the river rushes in two foaming leaps. Here in the gray of the morning we lugged our canoes and our camp-kit around the cataract, and then launched away for the end of our voyage. It was full of variety, for the river was now cutting its course through a series of ridges, and every mile was broken with rapids and larger falls. There was but one other place, however, where we had to make a portage. I believe it was called Grand Falls. After that, the stream was smooth and quiet. The tall maples and ashes and elms stood along the banks as if they had been planted for a park. The first faint touch of autumn colour was beginning to illuminate their foliage. A few weeks later the river would be a long, winding avenue of gold and crimson, for every tree would redouble its splendour in the dark, unruffled water.

At one place, where there were a few cleared fields bordering on the river, we saw two or three houses and barns, and supposed we were near the end of our voyage. This was about nine o'clock in the morning; and we were glad,

because we calculated that we could catch the
ten o'clock train for Bar Harbor. But that
calculation was far astray. We skirted the
cleared fields and entered the woodland again.
The river flowed, broad and leisurely, in great
curves half a mile long from point to point. As
we rounded one cape after another we said to
each other, "When we pass the next turn we
shall see the village." But that inconsiderate
village seemed to flee before us. Still the tall
trees lined the banks in placid monotony. Still
the river curved from cape to cape, each one
like all the others. We paddled hard and steadily. Ten o'clock passed. Every day of our
journey we had lost something—a frying-pan, a
hatchet, a paddle, a ring. This day was no
exception. We lost a train. Still we pushed
along against the cool wind, which always
headed us, whether we turned north, or east, or
south; wondering whether the village that we
sought was still in the world, wondering whether
the river came out anywhere, wondering—till at
last we saw, across a lake-like expanse of water,
the white church and the clustering houses of
the far-famed Whitneyville.

It was a quaint old town, which had seen better days. The big lumber-mill that had once
kept it busy was burned down, and the business

had slipped away to the prosperous neighbouring town of Machias. There were old houses
with tall pillars in front of them, now falling
into decay and slipping out of plumb. There
were shops that had evidently been closed for
years, with not even a sign "To Let" in the
windows. Our dinner was cooked for us in a
boarding-house, by a brisk young lady of about
fifteen years, whose mother had gone to Machias
for a day in the gay world. With one exception that pleasant young lady was the only
thing in Whitneyville that did not have an air
of having been left behind.

The exception was the establishment of Mr.
Cornelius D——, whose "General Store" beside
the bridge was still open for business, and whose
big white house stood under the elm-trees at
the corner of the road opposite the church, with
bright windows, fresh-painted walls, and plenty
of flowers blooming around it. He was walking
in the yard, dressed in a black broadcloth frock-
coat, with a black satin necktie and a collar
with pointed ends,—an old-fashioned Gladsto-
nian garb. When I heard him speak I knew
where he came from. It was the rich accent of
Killarney, just as I had heard it on the Irish
lakes two summers ago. But sixty years had
passed since the young Cornelius had left the

shores of the River Laune and come to dwell
by the Kowahshiscook. He had grown up with
the place; had run the lumber-mill and the first
railroad that hauled the lumber from the mill
down to tide-water; had become the owner of
the store and the proprietor of some sixteen
miles of timber-land along the river-front; had
built the chief house of the village and given his
children a capital education; and there he still
dwelt, with his wife from Killarney, and with
his tall sons and daughters about him, contented and happy, and not at all disposed to
question the beneficent order of the universe.
We had plenty of good talk that afternoon and
evening, chiefly about the Old Country, and I
had to rub up my recollections of Ross Castle
and Kenmare House and all the places around
Lough Leane, in order to match the old man's
memory. He was interested in our expedition,
too. He had often been far into the woods
looking after his lumber. But I doubt whether
he quite understood what it was that drew the
boy and me on our idle voyage from Nicatöus
to the sea.

HIS OTHER ENGAGEMENT

HIS OTHER ENGAGEMENT

AMONG the annals of the Petrine Club, which has for its motto the wise words of St. Peter, "I go a-fishing," there are several profitable tales. Next to the story of Beekman De Peyster's fatal success in transforming a fairly good wife into a ferocious angler, probably the most instructive is the singular adventure that befell Bolton Chichester in taking a brief vacation while he was engaged to be married. And having already told the former story as an example of the vicissitudes of *Fisherman's Luck*, I now propose to narrate the latter as a striking illustration of what may happen to a man who takes "a day off."

Chichester is known among his intimate friends as "Chinchin." This nominal appendix was given to him not in allusion to his habits of speech, for he is rather a small talker, but with reference to the prominence of that feature of his countenance which is at once the organ of utterance, the instrument of mastication, the sign of firmness, and (at least in the Gibsonian period of facial architecture) the chief point of manly beauty.

53

Point is an absurd word to apply to Chichester's chin. It might better be called a surface,
a region, a territory. Smooth, spacious, square,
kept always in perfect order and carried with a
what-do-I-care-for-that air, it gives him a most
distinguished appearance, and makes you think,
when you meet him, that you are in the pres-
ence of a favourite matinée actor, the hero of a
modern short-story, or a man of remarkable
decision of character.

The last, of course, is the correct interpreta-
tion of the sign. Bolton Chichester is the most
decided man that I have ever known. He can
make up his mind more quickly, on a greater
variety of subjects, and adhere to each determination more firmly, than all the other members of the Petrine Club put together. For this
reason we always anticipated for him a large
success in life, and some even predicted that he
would become President of the United States—
unless he made up his mind to do something
else on the way to the White House. At all
events, we felt sure, he would get what he
wanted; and when he became decidedly attentive to Ethel Asham it was taken for granted
that he would woo, win, and marry her in short
order.

She was rather a difficult person, to be sure;

the eldest daughter of that cryptic old millionaire, Watson Asham, who lived in New York
and resided, for purposes of taxation, at West
Smithfield; a graduate of Brainmore College;
president of the Social Settlement of Higher
Lighters; a frequent contributor in brief fiction
to the *Contrary Magazine;* a beauty of the tea-
after-tennis type; the best dancer in St. Swithin's
Lenten Circle, and the most romantic creature
that ever took up the cause of Progress with a
large P. It would not be fair to call her strong-
minded, because the adjective seems to imply
some kind of a limitation in her strength. She
was even stronger in her impulses than in her
mind; original in every direction; in fact, originality was a kind of convention with her. It
was wonderful how many things she accomplished; but then she never lost any time; she
was precise, punctual, inevitable in her sweet,
feminine, self-possessed way; and her varied
and surprising programme went through on
schedule time, while she cherished in her heart
the dream of a romance in the style of *The
Prisoner of Zenda.*

Naturally, such a many-sided young woman
would be difficult to please; and a number of
eligible young men had acquired personal knowledge of the fact. But the difficulty seemed to

attract Chichester. He went at it in his bold, decided manner, with his chin forward; and he conquered. After the February campaign no one was surprised to hear, in March, that the engagement of Miss Ethel Asham to Mr. Bolton Chichester was announced, and that the wedding would occur in June.

The place was not specified. Conjectures were hazarded that it might be Dunfermline Abbey, the Castle of Chillon, Bridal Veil Falls in the Yosemite, the Natural Bridge in Virginia, or St. George's, Hanover Square. Little Pop Wilson, the well-known dialect novelist of the southeastern part of northern Kentucky, suggested that there was something to be said in favor of the Mammoth Cave—"always cool, you know. Artificial lights, pulpit rock, stalactites—all that sort of thing!" Even this was felt to be within the bounds of possibility. The one thing that was not open to doubt was that the wedding would certainly be celebrated in an original way and a romantic place, at precisely the appointed hour. If anyone had foretold that it would be broken off, and that the reason given would be "another engagement" on the part of Mr. Bolton Chichester, we should have laughed in the face of such a ridiculous prophet and advised him to take something to cool his brain.

HIS OTHER ENGAGEMENT

Yet this is exactly what happened; and the secret of that other engagement is the subject of this brief, simple, but I hope not unmoral narrative.

Chichester had been with the Ashams at the residential farm-house in West Smithfield during the first fortnight of April, and had devoted the remainder of that showery month to his affairs in the city, diversified with a few afternoons of trout-fishing on Long Island: for like all the members of the Petrine Club he was a sincere angler. It was during this period that Ethel took up, in her daily correspondence with him, the question of the cruelty of angling. She was not yet quite clear in her mind upon the subject, but she wanted him to consider it seriously; and she quoted Byron, Leigh Hunt, and Aurora W. Chime's book, *The Inwardness of the Outward*. Chichester promised to consider it.

The second week in May they spent together at a house-party near Portland, Maine; and he tried the landlocked salmon in Sebago Lake, twice. Ethel continued the subject of the cruelty of angling, in conversation, and illuminated her increasing conviction with references to the Reverend Wilbur Short's *Tales of Strange Things in Woods and Waters*, and *Songs of the Scaly*, by Alonzo Sweetbread.

"You would not allow any difference of thought or feeling to mar the perfect chord of our love, would you, Bolton dear?" she asked.

"Of course not," said Bolton.

"Then promise me faithfully that you will think about this pastime which gives so much anguish to the innocent fish—think about it very, very seriously."

"I do. I have to. It costs me seven or eight hundred a year."

"But you must think in a different way. Put yourself in the place of the fish."

"I did once. Fellow with a rod and line tried to land me in the tank at the gymnasium. Lots of fun. Never had a better fight."

"But suppose you had a hook in your mouth. How would you like that?"

"Better than the dentist's chair, I'm sure. I spent three afternoons there, last month."

"You're absurd," said Ethel, "you're perverse. Don't hold your chin up in that aggravating way. I don't believe—you—love——"

The rest of the conversation followed the usual course, which may be supplied from the pages of any of the fifteen-cent magazines, and ended with a promise on the part of Chichester that he would think again, and very, very seriously.

HIS OTHER ENGAGEMENT

Meantime, you will understand, the preparations for the wedding had been going forward, in the regular way, modified, however, in one most important particular by Ethel Asham's passion for romantic originality. She insisted that the day and the place should be left entirely to her. She did not wish to have the ordinary, commonplace, fashionable wedding performance. She wanted something really and truly poetic and fitting, something to remember. She had a plan. The wedding should be in June? Yes. And she would be ready? Yes. And all the family, at least, should be there? Yes. But she asked that she might keep the secret of the precise time and the exact place as long as possible; it would make it all seem so much more spontaneous and natural.

The situation was a little peculiar, I grant you, and somewhat embarrassing to the rest of the family, including Chichester. But he took it like a man, and backed Ethel up with the utmost decision, just as if her idea was what he had always thought of and determined to do. What was his chin for, if he could not give her a firm support in a thing like this? As a matter of fact he did not care in the least where the wedding might be. A man never does. It does not seem to be his business. Ethel's paternal parent, however, had some misgivings which must be satisfied.

"Is it a church?" he growled; "none of your dusty, shabby little Higher Light shrines, eh?"

"Yes, it's a church," said Ethel solemnly, "and a very old and beautiful church."

"And a Christian ceremony," he insisted; "parson, robes, prayer-book—regular thing—no side-show performance, eh?"

"Of course," said she, "what do you think? Do you suppose that just because I see things in an original way, I don't know what's proper? I like to hear the Swami Abikadanda talk; and I don't want a regular cut-and-dried wedding; but I'm not going to take any risks about a thing like that. The clergyman will be there, and you will give me away, and Gladys and Victoria will be the bridesmaids, and Arthur will be the best man, and Howard and Willis——"

"Well, well," grunted her father, with his chuckling laugh, "it's all right, I suppose, seeing that it's your wedding. Have it your own way while you can." For the old man had formed his idea of the significance of Chichester's chin.

So it was settled that the affair should remain unsettled for every one except Ethel; and the whole family was plunged into a cheerful state

of evasion, prevarication, and downright falsifi-
cation; and Chichester grinned and smoothed
the left side of his chin with his forefinger and
said, "What do I care for that? It's all right,
I know," and everybody predicted that Ethel
Asham was about to do something very original.

In the middle of June she marshalled her
party for a little Canadian *giro*. There were her
father and mother; and the inseparable twins,
Gladys and Victoria, one of whom always
laughed when the other was amused; and the
three preternaturally important brothers, representing the triple-x output of Harvard, Yale
and Columbia; and Aunt Euphemia van Benschoten, who had inherited the van Benschoten
nose, a block on Fifth Avenue, and a pew in St.
Mark's church (two of which possessions she
was entitled to devise by will); and Miss Nancy
Bangs, Ethel's most intimate friend; and the
Reverend Oriel Bellingham Jenks, her favourite
clergyman of the period; and—oh, yes! of course
—there was Bolton Chichester.

It was quite a large party. They went first
to Niagara, which Pop Wilson said was "premature, if not improper." Then they went
down through the Thousand Islands, where
Ethel pointed out the inhuman and cruel expression of the many fishermen, to which Chichester

answered, "I don't know that it's cruel to catch pickerel, but it's certainly childish."

Then they descended the ridiculous rapids of Lachine, which splashed and murmured around them like a very mild surf at Shelter Island. They spent a couple of days in looking for the antiquities of Montreal, trying to find the romantic atmosphere of New France under the *ancien régime*. Then they went to Quebec, and found it.

Dear, delightful old Quebec, with her gray walls and shining tin roofs; her precipitous, headlong streets and sleepy squares and esplanades; her narrow alleys and peaceful convents; her harmless antique cannon on the parapets and her sweet-toned bells in the spires; her towering château on the heights and her long, low, queer-smelling warehouses in the lower town; her spick-and-span *caléches* and her dingy trolley-cars; her sprinkling of soldiers and sailors with Scotch accent and Irish brogue and Cockney twang, on a background of *petite bourgeoisie* speaking the quaintest of French dialects; her memories of an adventurous, glittering past and her placid contentment with the tranquil grayness of the present; her glorious daylight outlook over the vale of the St. Charles, the level shore of Montmorenci, the green Isle d'Orleans dividing the shining reaches of the broad St. Lawrence, and the blue Laurentian Mountains rolling far to the eastward—and at night, the dark bulk of the Citadel outlined against the starry blue, the trampling of many feet up and down the wooden pavement of Dufferin Terrace, the chattering and the laughter, the music of the military band, and far below, the huddled housetops, the silent wharves, the lights of the ships swinging with the tide, the intermittent ferry-boats plying to and fro, the twinkling lamps of Levis rising along the dim southern shore and reflected in the lapsing, curling, seaward-sliding waves of the great river! What city of the New World keeps so much of the charm of the Old?

The camp which Samuel de Champlain made in the wilderness three hundred years ago, has become one of the last refuges of the romantic dream and the courtly illusion, still haunted by the shades of impecunious young noblemen with velvet cloaks and feathered hats and rapiers at their hips; of delicate, high-spirited beauties braving the snowy wildwood in their silks and laces; of missionary monks, tonsured and rope-girdled, pressing with lean faces and eager eyes to plant the banner of the Church upon the shores of the West and win the fiery crown of martyrdom. Other figures follow them—gold-

63

seekers, fur-traders, empire-builders, admirals and generals of France and England, strugglers for dominion, soldiers of fortune, makers of cunning plots, and dreamers of great enterprises—and round them all flows the confused tide of war and love, of intrigue and daring, of religious devotion and imperial plot. The massive walls of the old city have been broken, the rude palaces have vanished in fire or sunken in decay, but the past is still indomitable on Cape Diamond, and the lovers of romance can lose themselves in pleasant reveries among the winding streets and on the lofty, sun-bathed ramparts of Quebec.

It was there, in a shady corner of the Grand Battery, that Ethel disclosed to her mother and Chichester and the Reverend Father Bellingham Jenks her plan for the wedding; since, indeed, it was hardly possible to keep it a secret any longer.

"The day after to-morrow, you know," said she, "we are going to take the Saguenay boat for Tadousac. Do you know that village curving along the cliff at the base of the Mamelons; and the half-circle of the bay opening out into the big St. Lawrence, full of sunshine and blue water; and the steep, shaggy mountains of the Saguenay in the background; and the tiny old

64

mission chapel of the Jesuit Fathers where the same bell has been ringing for nearly three hundred years? I was there the summer after I graduated; and I've never forgotten it. It's a picture and a dream. That is where I want to have my wedding. I don't believe that anybody else would have thought of it. Perhaps it's more than a hundred years since the last Indian wedding was held in that little deserted chapel; but it's all right, kept in good order, just as a relic beside the big new church. I think"—turning to the clergyman—"that it will be perfectly delightful and original to have you marry me there, at high noon, on the last day of June."

Well, of course, there was a good deal of astonishment and confusion and reluctance when this extraordinary plan came out. No one had imagined precisely this turn in Ethel's originality. Her mother was in a state of paralyzed dismay at an idea so wildly unconventional; the twins and her brothers and Miss Nancy Bangs bubbled over with practical difficulties and protests; Father Bellingham Jenks was doubtful and embarrassed. "Would it be possible—decorous—regular? The Roman Branch, you know, has not yet openly acknowledged the Anglican position in The Church.

Might not objections arise—misunderstanding—
refusal of permission to use the chapel? I
should hesitate very much, you know!"

But Ethel carried things through with her
usual sweet, sparkling high-handedness; and
Chichester supported her with irresistible determination, as if he had decided on exactly this
thing years ago.

"Certainly," he said, "splendid idea—entirely
novel—quite correct—nothing could be better.
Telegraph for one wing of the Tadousac Hotel,
with drawing-rooms and private dining-room.
Send down plenty of flowers and cakes and
wines and whatever we need from here by boat
on the twenty-ninth. Get a letter of introduc-
tion from my friend Paradol, the Minister of
Fisheries and Lighthouses, to the archbishop
here—letter from him to the curé at Tadousac
—keys of the chapel—permission to make draw-
ings and photographs of the interior every
morning of next week. I've been at Tadousac
almost every summer for the last five or six
years, on the way to my salmon-fishing at the
Ste. Marjorie Club. It's all perfectly easy and
it shall be done."

The difficulties seemed to vanish before his
masterful air, and everybody fell into line with
sudden enthusiasm. Ethel smiled discreetly and

moved along her pathway of inflexible originality with gentle triumph. The voyage down the river was delightful. The arrangements at the big white wooden hotel on the curving bay were rather primitive but quite comfortable; and three of the five days which were to pass before the ringing of the antique wedding-bell slipped away as if by magic.

On the fourth day, June twenty-ninth, Chichester, having been assured by telegraph that all the things from Quebec had been safely shipped on the *Ste. Irenée*, was spending a morning hour with Ethel in the pavilion of the Government Fish Station at *Anse à l'Eau*, watching the great herd of captive salmon, circling round and round in restless imprisonment in their warm shallow pool. The splendid fish were growing a little dull and languid in their confined quarters, freshened only by the inflowing of a small brook, and exposed to the full glare of the sun. Many of them bore the scars of the nets in which they had been captured. Others had red wounds on the ends of their noses where they had butted against the rocks or the timbers of the dam. There were some hundreds of the fish, and every now and then a huge thirty-pounder would wallow on top of the water, or a small, lively one would spring high into the air and fall back with a sounding splash on his side. Here they must wait through the summer, the pool becoming daily hotter, more crowded, more uncomfortable, until the time came when the hatchery men would strip them of their spawn. To an angler the sight was somewhat depressing, though he might admit the strength of the arguments for the artificial propagation of fish. But to Ethel it seemed a pretty spectacle and a striking contrast to the cruelty of angling.

"Look at them," she said, "how happy they are, and how safe! No fly-fishermen to stick a hook in their mouths and make them suffer. How can you bear to do it?"

"Well," said Chichester, "if it comes to suffering, I doubt whether the fish are conscious of any such thing, as we understand it. But even if they are, they suffer twice as much, and a thousand times as long, shut up in this hot, nasty pool, as they would in being caught in proper style."

"But think of the hook!"

"Hurts about as much as a pin-prick."

"But think of the fearful struggle, and the long, gasping agony on the shore."

"There's no fear in the struggle; it's just a trial of strength and skill, like a game of football. A fish doesn't know anything about death; so he has no fear of it. And there is no gasping on the shore; nothing but a quick rap on the head with a stick, and it's all over."

"But why should he be killed at all?"

"Well," said he, smiling, "there are reasons of taste. You eat salmon, don't you?"

"Ye-e-es," she answered a little doubtfully—then with more assurance, "but remember what Wilbur Short says in that lovely chapter on 'Communion with the Catfish': I want them brought to the table in the simplest and most painless way."

"And that is angling with the fly," said he, still more decidedly. "The fly is not swallowed like a bait. It sticks in the skin of the lip where there is least feeling. There is no torture in the play of a salmon. It's just a fair fight with an unknown opponent. Compare it with the other ways of bringing a fish to the table. If he's caught in a net he hangs there for hours, slowly strangled. If he's speared, half the time the spear slips and he struggles off badly wounded; and if the spear goes through him, he is flung out on the bank to bleed to death. Even if he escapes, he is sure to come to a pitiful end some day—perish by starvation when he gets too old to catch his food—or be torn to pieces by a

69

seal, an otter, or a fish-hawk. Fly-fishing really offers him——"

"Never mind that," said Ethel, "what does it offer you?"

"A gentleman's sport, I suppose," he answered rather slowly. "That is, a fair and exciting effort to get something that is made for human use, in a way that involves some hardship, a little risk, a good deal of skill and patience and perseverance, and plenty of out-of-door life. I guess it must be an inheritance of the old days when people lived by the chase; but, whatever it is, almost every real man feels a certain kind of gratification in being able to get game or fish by the exertion of his own pluck or skill. Some day perhaps this will all be changed, and we shall be contented to take our exercise in the form of massage or croquet, and our food in compressed tablets. But not yet!"

Ethel shook her head and smiled rather sadly. "Bolton," she said, "you discourage me. You argue in this way because you like fishing."

"I do," he answered, promptly. "And so far as I can see, that is the principal reason why your friends, Aurora W. Chime and the Reverend Wilbur Short, and the rest of them, condemn it. They object to the evident pleasure

of the fisherman more than to the imaginary
suffering of the fish."

"Bolton!" she exclaimed earnestly, "that is
not a fair thing to say. They are truly good
and noble teachers. They live on a lofty plane
and labour for the spreading of the Higher
Light. You will know them when we are married. They will be far better company for you
than the thoughtless fishermen in your clubs."

Bolton looked a little glum. But he behaved
like a gentleman, and cheered up. "Well, well,"
he said, "of course—you know—your friends,
my friends! I'll be glad to meet them, and
hear what they have to say, and consider it all
very, very seriously. I promised you that,
dearest, you remember. But that reminds me
—there are two of the men on the *Ste. Marjorie*
now, at the club-house—Colonel Lang and the
Doctor—old Harvey, you know—fine old chap.
It's only twenty miles away. Couldn't we send
word to them and ask them to come down for
to-morrow? I'm so proud and happy about it
all; I'd like to have them here, if you don't
mind."

"Why, certainly," she answered, smiling with
manifest pleasure, "that will be delightful.
We'll send a messenger at once with a note to
them. But stop a moment—I have a better

71

plan than that! Why not drive over yourself,
this afternoon, to invite them? You'll be glad
to see them again; and if you stay here you'll
only be in the way until to-morrow," laughed
she. "Why not go over and spend the night at
the club-house and come back early in the
morning? That will be quite like the ancient
days—the young adventurer hurrying out of
the forest to meet his bride."

Bolton insisted that he couldn't think of it—
didn't want to go—would much rather stay
where he was. But Ethel was captivated with
the novelty of the idea. She always liked her
own plans. Besides, she really wished to have
him out of the way for the rest of the day and
the evening. There was a good deal to be done
—letters to be written—a long, personal, uplift-
ing talk with Nancy Bangs, and with Gladys,
and with Victoria, and with each of her brothers
separately—just half-an-hour of soul-counsel for
each one: three hours altogether. She would
see them in regular succession, beginning with
the youngest brother, and winding up with
Nancy. Then she was charmed with the picture of Bolton coming in, post haste, in the
morning, as if he had just arrived from a journey across the great northern wilderness. So
she carried her point, and when he had agreed

to it, he found that he rather liked the plan too. It gave him something to do, a chance to practise his habit of putting things through with determination.

He sent a messenger over to *Sacré Cœur* at once, to say that he was coming and that a canoe should meet him at the landing-place on the North-East Branch. He finished up all the arrangements that remained to be made at Tadousac for the smooth running of to-morrow's affair. He ordered a good horse and a "*quatre roue*" to be ready for him at five o'clock; and having parted with Ethel in the manner appropriate even for so brief a separation, he got away for the river in due season.

The long road with its heavy stretches of sand, its incredibly steep clay hills, its ruts and bumpers over which the buckboard rocked like a boat in a choppy sea, and its succession of shadeless *habitant* houses and discouraged farms, had never seemed to him so monotonous. At eight o'clock, when it was growing dusk, and the moon rising, he reached the landing-place on the Branch, and found his canoe, with his two old canoe-men, P'tit Louis, and Vieux Louis, waiting for him. With their warm, homely greeting his spirits began to revive; and the swift run through foaming rapids and eddying pools, along the three miles of the Branch, brought him into a state of mind that was thoroughly cheerful, not to say exhilarated. There was Brackett's Camp on the point above the Forks; and there was the veteran painter-angler himself, with his white beard and his knickerbockers, standing on the shore to wave a salutation as the canoe shot by the point. There was the main river, rushing down with full waters from the northwest, and roaring past the island. There was the club-house among the white birches and the balsams on the opposite bank, with the two flags fluttering in the moonlight, and the lights twinkling from the long, low veranda. And there were half a dozen canoe-men with a lantern at the landing-steps, and old John the steward in his white apron rubbing his hands, and the Colonel and the Doctor blowing the conch and the fish-horn in merry welcome. It was all very jolly, and Chichester knew at once that he was at home.

Dinner at nine o'clock, before the big open hearth, with a friendly fire. Much chaffing and pleasant talk about the arrangements for to-morrow. A man to be sent off at daybreak to have two buckboards ready at the landing at seven for the drive to Tadousac. Then a reprehensible quantity of tobacco smoked in the book-room, and the tale of the season's angling told from the beginning with many embellishments and divagations. There were stories of good luck and bad; vituperations of the lumbermen for leaving tree-tops and broken branches in the stream to get caught among the rocks and ruin the fishing; accounts of the immense number of salmon that had been seen leaping in the estuary, waiting to come up the river. The interest centred in the story of a huge fish that had taken up his transient abode in the pool called *La Fourche*. The Colonel had pricked and lost the monster two days ago, and had seen him jump twice yesterday. The Colonel was greatly excited about it, and vowed it was the largest salmon seen in the river for ten years—"a whale, I tell you, a regular *marsouin!* " he cried, waving his hands in the air. The Doctor was provokingly sceptical about the size of the fish. But both agreed that there was one thing that must be done. Chichester must try a few casts in *La Fourche* early in the morning.

"Yes," said the Doctor, puffing slowly at his pipe, "plenty of time between daylight and breakfast—good hour for a shy, old fish—we give up our rights to you—the pool is yours—see what you can do with it—may be your last chance to try your luck—" for somehow a rumour in regard to Miss Asham's views on angling had leaked out, and Chichester's friends were inclined to make merry about it.

He rose to the fly decidedly. "I don't know about this being my last chance," said he, "but I'll take it, any way. John, give me a call at four sharp, and tell the two Louis to be ready with the canoe and the rod and the big landing-net."

The little wreaths of grey mist were curling up from the river, and the fleecy western clouds were tinged with wild rose behind the wooded hills, as Chichester stepped out on the slippery rocks at the head of the pool, loosened his line, gave a couple of pulls to his reel to see that the click was all right, waved his slender rod in the air, and sent his fly out across the swift current. Once it swung around, dancing over the water, without result. The second cast carried it out a few feet further, and it curved through a wider arc, but still without result. The third cast sent it a little further still, past the edge of a big sunken rock in the current. There was a flash of silver in the amber water, a great splash on the surface, a broad tail waved in the air and vanished—an immense salmon had risen and missed the fly.

76

HIS OTHER ENGAGEMENT

Chichester reeled in his line and sat down. His pulses were hammering, and his chin was set at the angle of solid determination. "The Colonel was right," he said, "that's an enormous fish, *and he's mine!*"

He waited the full five minutes, according to ancient rule, before making the next cast. There was a tiny wren singing among the Balm-o'-Gilead trees on the opposite shore, with a voice that rose silverly above the noise of the rapids. "Cheer up, cheer up," it seemed to say, "what's the matter with you? Don't hurry, don't worry, try it again—again—again!"

But the next cast was made in vain. There was no response. Chichester changed his fly. The result was the same. He tried three different flies in succession without effect. Then he gave the top of the pool a rest, and fished down through the smooth water at the lower end, hooking and losing a small fish. Then he came back to the big salmon again, and fished a small Durham Ranger over him without success. A number four Critchley's Fancy produced no better result. A tiny double Silver Grey brought no response. Then he looked through his fly-box in despair, and picked out an old two-nought Prince of Orange—a huge, gaudy affair with battered feathers, which he had used two years be-

77

fore in flood-water on the Restigouche. At
least it would astonish the salmon, for it looked
like a last season's picture-hat, very much the
worse for wear. It lit on the ripples with a
splash, and floated down stream in a dishevelled
state till it reached the edge of the sunken rock.
Bang! The salmon rose to that incredible fly
with a rush, and went tearing across the pool.

The reel shrieked wildly as the line ran out.
The rod quivered and bent almost double. Chichester had the butt pressed against his belt,
the tip well up in the air, the reel-handle free
from any possible touch of coat-flap or sleeve.
To check that fierce rush by a hundredth part
of a second meant the snapping of the delicate
casting-line, or the smashing of the pliant rod-
tip. He knew, as the salmon leaped clear of
the water, once, twice, three times, that he was
in for the fight of his life; and he dropped the
point of the rod quickly at each leap to yield to
the sudden strain.

The play, at first, was fast and furious. The
salmon started up the stream, breasting the
rapids at a lively rate, and taking out line as
rapidly as the reel could run. Chichester followed along the open shore, holding his rod high
with both hands, stumbling over the big rocks,
wading knee-deep across a side-channel of the

river, but keeping his feet somehow, until the
fish paused in the lower part of the pool called
La Batture. Here there was a chance to reel in
line, and the men poled the canoe up from
below, to be ready for the next turn in the contest.

The salmon was now sulking at the bottom,
with his head down, balanced against the current, and boring steadily. He kept this up for
a quarter of an hour, then made a rush up the
pool, and a sidelong skittering leap on the surface. Coming back with a sudden turn, he
threw a somersault in the air, close to the opposite shore, sank to the bottom and began jigging. Jig, jig, jig, from side to side, with short,
heavy jerks, he worked his way back and forth
twice the length of the pool. Chichester knew
it was dangerous. Any one of these sharp blows
might snap the leader or the hook. But he
couldn't stop it. There was nothing to do but
wait, with tense nerves, until the salmon got
through jigging.

The change came suddenly. A notion to go
down stream struck the salmon like a flash of
lightning; without a moment's warning he took
the line over his shoulder and darted into the
rapids. *"Il va descendre! Vite, vite! Le ca-
not! Au large!"* shouted the two Louis; but

Chichester had already stepped into his place in the middle of the canoe, and there were still forty yards of white line left on the reel, when the narrow boat dashed away in pursuit of the fish, impelled by flashing paddles and flinging the spray to right and left. There were many large rocks half hidden in the wild white water through which they were plunging, and with a long line there was danger that the fish would take a turn around one of them and break away. It was necessary to go faster than he went, in order to retrieve as much line as possible. But paddle as fast as they could the fish kept ahead. He was not towing the boat, of course; for only an ignoramus imagines that a salmon can "tow" a boat, when the casting-line that holds him is a single strand of gut that will break under a strain of ten pounds. He was running away, and the canoe was chasing him through the roaring torrent. But he held his lead, and there were still eighty or ninety yards of line out when he rushed down the last plunge into *La Fourche.*

The situation was this: The river here is shaped like a big Y. The salmon went down the inside edge of the left-hand fork. The canoe followed him down the outside edge of the same fork. When he came to the junction it was natural to suppose that he would follow the current down the main stem of the Y. But instead of that, when the canoe dropped into the comparative stillness of the pool, the line was stretched, taut and quivering, across the foot of the left-hand fork and straight up into the current of the right-hand fork. "He's gone up the other branch," shouted Chichester, above the roar of the stream, "we must follow him! Push across the rapids! Push lively!" So the men seized their setting-poles and shoved as fast as they could across the foot of the rapids, while the rushing torrent threatened at every moment to come in over the side and swamp the canoe. There was a tugging and a trembling on the line, and it led, apparently, up the North-East Branch, past Brackett's Camp. But when the canoe reached the middle of the rapids P'tit Louis uttered an exclamation, leaned over the bow, and pulled up the end of a tree-top, the butt of which was firmly wedged among the rocks. Around the slender branches, waving and quivering in the current with life-like motion, the line was looped. The lower part of it trailed away loosely down the stream into the pool.

Chichester took in the situation in a flash of grieved insight. "Well," he said, "that is positively the worst! Good-by, Mr. Salmon. Louis, pull out that-er, er—that branch!" and he began slowly to reel in the line. But old Louis, in the stern of the canoe, had taken hold of the slack and was pulling it in hand over hand. In a second he shouted "*Arrêtez! Arrêtez! M'sieu, il n'est pas parti, il est la!*"

It was a most extraordinary affair. The spring of the flexible branch had been enough to keep the line from breaking. The salmon, resting in the comparatively still water of the pool, had remained at the end of the slack, and the hook, by some fortunate chance, held firm. It took but a moment to get the line taut and the point of the rod up again. And then the battle began anew. The salmon was refreshed by his fifteen minutes between the halves of the game. No centre in a rush-line ever played harder or faster.

He exhausted the possibilities of attack and defence in *La Fourche*, and then started down the rapids again. In the little pot-hole in mid-river, called *Pool à Michel*, he halted; but it was only for a minute. Soon he was flying down the swift water, the canoe after him, toward the fierce, foaming channel which runs between the island and the eastern bank opposite the club-house. Chichester could see the Colonel and the Doctor at the landing, waving and beckoning to him, as he darted along with the current. Intent upon carrying his fight through to a finish, he gave only a passing glance to what he thought was their friendly gesture of encouragement, took his right hand from the reel for a second to wave a greeting, and passed on, with determination written in every line of his chin, following the fish toward the sea.

Through the clear shallows of *La Pinette*, and the rapids below; through the curling depths of *Pool à Pierre*, and the rapids below; through the long, curving reach of *L'Hirondelle*, and the mad rapids below; so the battle went, and it was fight, fight, fight, and never the word "give up!" At last they came to the head of tide-water and the lake-like pool beside the old quay. Here the methods of the fish changed. There was no more leaping in the air; no more violent jigging; no more swift rushing up or down stream; but instead, there was just an obstinate adherence to the deepest water in the pool, a slow and steady circling round and round in some invisible eddy below the surface. From this he could only be moved by pressure. Now was the time to test the strength of the rod and line. The fish was lifted a few feet by main force, and the line reeled in while the rod was lowered again. Then there was another lift, and another reeling in; and so the process was repeated until he was brought close to the shore in comparatively shallow water. Even yet he did not turn over on his back, or show the white fin; but it was evident that he was through fighting.

Chichester and P'tit Louis stepped out on the shore, old Louis holding the canoe. P'tit Louis made his way carefully to a point of rock, with the wide-mouthed, long-handled net, and dipped it quietly down into the water, two or three feet deep. The fish was guided gently in toward the shore, and allowed to drop back with the smooth current until the net was around him. Then it was swiftly lifted; there was the gleam of an immense mass of silver in its meshes, an instant of furious struggle, the quick stroke of a short, heavy *baton;* and the great salmon was landed and despatched.

The hook was well set in the outside of his jaw, just underneath his chin; no wonder he played so long, with his mouth shut! Bring the spring-balance and test his weight. Forty-eight pounds, full measure, the record salmon of the river—a deep thickset fish, whose gleaming silver sides and sharp teeth proved him fresh-run from the sea! It was a signal victory for an angler to land such a fish under such conditions, and Chichester felt that fortune had been with him.

He enjoyed a quarter of an hour of great satisfaction as the men poled the canoe up-river to the club-house. But there was a shadow of anxiety, of vague misgiving, that troubled him; and he urged the men to make haste. At the landing the Colonel and the Doctor were waiting, with strange, long, inscrutable faces.

"Did you get him?" they said.

"I did," he answered; "forty-eight pounds. Hold up that fish, Louis!"

"Magnificent," they cried, "a great fish! You've done it! But, man, do you know what time it is? Five minutes to ten o'clock!"

Nearly ten, and twenty miles of rough river and road to cover before high noon. Was it possible? In a second it flashed upon Chichester what he had done, what a fearful situation he must face. "Come on, you fellows," he cried, stepping back into the canoe. "Now, Louis, shove her as you never shoved before! Ten dollars apiece if you make the upper landing in half an hour."

The other canoe followed immediately. They found the two buckboards waiting, and scrambled in, explaining to the drivers the necessity for the utmost haste. Chichester's horse was a

scrawny, speedy little beast, called *Le Coq Noir*,
the champion trotter of the region. "*Hé,
Coq!*" shouted the driver, flourishing his whip,
at the top of the first long hill; and they started
off at a breakneck pace. They passed through
the village of *Sacré Cœur* a mile and a half ahead
of the other wagon. But on the first steep *côte*
beyond the village, the inevitable happened.
The buckboard went slithering down the slippery slope of clay, struck a log bridge at the
bottom with a resounding thump, and broke
an axle clean across. The wheel flew off, and
the buckboard came to the ground, and Chichester and the driver tumbled out. The Black
Cock gave a couple of leaps and then stood still,
looking back with an expression of absolute
dismay.

There was nothing to do but wait for the
other buckboard, which arrived in ten or fifteen
minutes. "Will you have the kindness to lend
me your carriage?" said Chichester elaborately.
"Oh, don't talk! Get out quick. You can
walk!" They changed horses quickly, and
Chichester took the reins and drove on. Quarter past eleven; half past; twenty minutes to
twelve—and three miles yet to go! It was
barely possible to do it. And perhaps it would
have been done, if at that moment the good lit-

tle Black Cock had not stumbled on a loose stone, gone down almost to his knees, and recovered himself with a violent wrench—lame! Chichester was a fair runner and a good walker. But he knew that the steep sandy hills which lay between him and Tadousac could never be covered in twenty minutes. He gave the reins to the driver, leaned back in the seat, and folded his arms.

At twenty-five minutes past twelve the buckboard passed slowly down the main street of Tadousac, bumped deliberately across the bridge, and drew up before the hotel. The little white chapel on the other side of the road was shut, deserted, sleeping in the sunlight. On the long hotel piazza were half a dozen groups of strangers, summer visitors, evidently in a state of suppressed curiosity and amusement. They fell silent as the disconsolate vehicle came to a halt, and Arthur Asham, the Harvard brother, in irreproachable morning costume and perfect form, moved forward to meet it.

"Well?" said Chichester, as he stepped out.

"Well!" answered the other; and they went a few paces together on the lawn, shaking hands politely and looking at each other with unspoken interrogations.

"I'm awfully sorry," Chichester said, "but it

87

couldn't be helped. A chapter of accidents—I'll explain."

"My dear fellow," answered young Asham, "what good will that do? You needn't explain to me, and you can't explain to Ethel. She is in her most lofty and impossible mood. She'll never listen to you. I'm awfully sorry, too, but I fear it's all over. In fact, she has driven down to the wharf with the others to wait for the Quebec boat, which goes at one. I am staying to get the luggage together and bring it on to-morrow. She gave me this note for you. Will you read it?"

Asham politely turned away, and Chichester read:

"MY DEAR MR. CHICHESTER:

"Fortunate indeed is the disillusion which does not come too late. But the bridegroom who comes too late is known in time.

"You may be sure that I have no resentment at what you have done; I have risen to those heights where anger is unknown. But I now see clearly what I have long felt dimly—that your soul does not keep time with the music to which my life is set. I do not know what *other engagement* kept you away. I do not ask to know. I know only that ours is at an end, and

88

you are at liberty to return to your fishing. That you will succeed in it is the expectation of

"Your well-wisher

"E. Asham."

Chichester's chin dropped a little as he read. For the first time in his life he looked undecided. Then he folded the note carefully, put it in the breast pocket of his coat, and turned to his companion.

"You will be going up in to-morrow's boat, I suppose. Shall we go together?"

"My dear fellow," said Arthur Asham, "really, you know—I should be delighted. But do you think it would be quite the thing?"

BOOKS THAT I LOVED
AS A BOY

BOOKS THAT I LOVED
AS A BOY

"IT is one thing," said my Uncle Peter, "to be perfectly honest. But it is quite another thing to tell the truth."

"Are you honest in that remark," I asked, "or are you merely telling the truth?"

"Both," he answered, with twinkling eyes, "for that is an abstract remark, in which species of discourse truth-telling is comparatively easy. Abstract remarks are a great relief to the lazy honest man. They spare him the trouble of meticulous investigation of unimportant facts. But a concrete remark, touching upon a number of small details, is full of traps for the truth-teller."

"You agree, then," said I, "with what the Psalmist said in his haste: 'All men are liars'?"

"Not in the least," he replied, laying down the volume which he was apparently reading when he interrupted himself. "I have leisure enough to perceive at once the falsity of that observation which the honest Psalmist recorded for our amusement. The real liars, conscious, malicious, wilful falsifiers, must always be a minority in the world, because their habits tend to bring them to an early grave or a reformatory. It is the people who want to tell the truth, and try to, but do not quite succeed, who are in the majority. Just look at this virtuous little volume which I was reading when you broke in upon me. It is called *Books that Have Influenced Me.* A number of authors, politicians, preachers, doctors, and rich men profess to give an account of the youthful reading which has been most influential in the development of their mature minds and characters. To judge from what they have written here you would suppose that these men were as acute and discriminating at sixteen as they are at sixty. They tell of great books, serious books, famous books. But they say little or nothing of the small, amusing books, the books full of fighting and adventure, the books of good stuff poorly written, in which every honest boy, at some time in his life, finds what he wants. They are silent, too, about the books which as a matter of fact had a tremendous influence on them—the plain, dull school-books. For my part, if you asked me what books had influenced me, I should not be telling the truth if my answer left out Webster's Spelling-Book

and Greenleaf's Arithmetic, though I did not
adore them extravagantly."

"That's just the point, Uncle Peter," said I,
"these distinguished men were really trying to
tell you about the books that delighted and inspired their youth, the books that they loved as
boys."

"Well," said my Uncle Peter, "if it comes to
love, and reminiscences of loving, that is precisely the region in which the exact truth is least
frequently told. Maturity casts its prim and
clear-cut shadow backwards upon the vague
and glittering landscape of youth. Whether he
speaks of books or of girls, the aged reminiscent
attributes to himself a delicacy of taste, a sin-
gleness and constancy of affection, and a romantic fervour of devotion, which he might have
had, but probably did not. He is not in the
least to blame for drawing his fancy-picture of
a young gentleman. He cannot help it. It is
his involuntary tribute to the ideal. Youth
dreams in the future tense; age in the past par-
ticiple.

"There is no kind of fiction more amiable and
engaging than the droll legends of infancy and
pious recollections of boyhood. Do you suppose that Wordsworth has given us a complete
portrait of the boy that he was, in *The Pre-*

lude? He says not a word about the picture
of his grandmother that he broke with his whip
because the other children gave him a 'dare,'
nor about the day when he went up into the
attic with an old fencing-foil to commit suicide,
nor about the girl with whom he fell in love
while he was in France. Do you suppose that
Stevenson's *Memories and Portraits* represent
the youthful R. L. S. with photographic accu-
racy and with all his frills? Not at all. Stevenson's essays are charming; and Wordsworth's
poem is beautiful,—in streaks it is as fine as
anything that he ever wrote: but both of these
works belong to literature because they are
packed full of omissions,—which Stevenson himself called 'a kind of negative exaggeration.'
No, my dear boy, old Goethe found the right
title for a book of reminiscences when he wrote
Wahrheit und Dichtung. Truth and poetry,—
that is what it is bound to be. I don't know
whether Goethe was as honest a man as Wordsworth and Stevenson, but I reckon he told
about as much of the truth. Autobiography is
usually a man's view of what his biography
ought to be."

"This is rather a disquieting thought, my
Uncle Peter," said I, "for it seems to leave us
all adrift on a sea of illusions."

BOOKS THAT I LOVED AS A BOY

"Not if you look at it in the right way," he answered, placidly. "We can always get at a few more facts than the man himself gives us, from letters and from the dispassionate recollections of his friends. Besides, a man's view of what his life ought to have been is almost as interesting, and quite as instructive, as a mere chronicle of what it actually was. The truth is, there are two kinds of truth: one kind is——"

Crash! went the fire-irons, tumbling in brazen confusion on the red-brick hearth. When my Uncle Peter has mounted his favourite metaphysical theory, I know that nothing can make him dismount but physical violence. I apologized for the poker and the shovel and the tongs (practising a Stevensonian omission in regard to my own share in the catastrophe), arranged the offending members in their proper station on the left of the fire-place, and took the bellows to encourage the dull fire into a more lively flame.

"I know enough about the different kinds of truth," said I, working away at the bellows. "Haven't I just been reading Professor Jacobus on *Varieties of Psychic Experience*? What I want now is something concrete; and I wish you would try to give it to me, whatever perils it may involve. Tell me something about the books that you loved as a boy. Never mind your veracity, Uncle Peter, just be honest, that will be enough."

"My veracity!" he grunted. "Humph! Impudent academic mocker, university life has destroyed your last rag of reverence. You have become a mere pivot for turning another fellow's remarks against himself. However, if you will just allow me to talk, and promise to let those fire-irons alone, I will tell you about some of the literary loves of my boyhood."

"I promise not to stir hand or tongue or foot," said I, "unless I see you sliding towards a metaphysical precipice."

"Very well," said my Uncle Peter, "I will do my best to give you the facts. And the first is this: there never was a day in my boyhood when I would not rather go a-fishing than read the best book in the world. If the choice had been given me, I never would have hesitated between climbing a mountain or paddling a canoe, and spending hours in a library. I would have liked also to hunt grizzly bears and to fight Indians,—but these were purely Platonic passions, detached from physical experience. I never realized them in hot blood.

"My native preferences were trimmed and pruned by the fortune that fixed my abode, during nine months of every year, in the city of Brooklyn, where there were no mountains to climb, no rivers to explore and no bears to hunt. The winter of my discontent, however, was somewhat cheered by games of football and baseball in the vacant lots on the heights above Wall Street Ferry, and by fierce battles and single combats with the tribes of 'Micks' who inhabited the regions of Furman Street and Atlantic Avenue. There was no High Court of Arbitration to suggest a peaceful solution of the difficulties out of which these conflicts arose. In fact, so far as I can remember, there was seldom a *casus belli* which could be defined and discussed. The warfare simply effervesced, like gas from a mineral spring. It was chronic, geographical, temperamental, and its everlasting continuance was suggested in the threat with which the combatants usually parted: 'wait till we ketch you alone, down our street!'

"There was also a school, the Brooklyn Polytechnic, which claimed some hours of my attention on five days of the week. On holidays my father used to take me on the most delightful fishing excursions to the then unpolluted waters of Coney Island Creek and Sheepshead Bay; and on Monday afternoons in midwinter it was a regular thing that I should go with him to

99

New York to ramble among the old book-shops in Nassau Street and eat oysters at Dorlon's stall, with wooden tables and sawdust-sprinkled floor, in Fulton Market. Say what you please about the friendship of books: it was worth a thousand times more to have the friendship of such a father.

"But there was still a good deal of unoccupied time on my hands between the first of October and the first of May, and having learned to read (in the old-fashioned way, by wrestling with the alphabet and plain spelling), at the age of about five years, I was willing enough to give some of my juvenile leisure to books and try to find out what they had to say about various things which interested me. I did not go to school until my tenth year, and so there was quite a long period left free for general reading, beginning with the delightful old-fashioned books of fairy tales without a moral, and closing with *Robinson Crusoe*, *Don Quixote*, and Plutarch's *Lives of Illustrious Men*. In the last two books I took a real and vivid interest, though I now suspect that it was strictly limited in range. They seemed to open a new world to me, the world of the past, in which I could see men moving about and doing the most remarkable things. Both of these books appeared to

100

me equally historical; I neither doubted the truth of their narratives nor attended to the philosophical reflections with which they were padded. The meaning of the long words I guessed at.

"My taste at this time was most indiscriminate. I could find some kind of enjoyment in almost anything that called itself a book—even a Sunday-school story, or a child's history of the world—provided only it gave something concrete for imagination to work upon. The mere process of reading, with the play of fancy that it quickened, became an agreeable pastime. I got a great deal of pleasure, and possibly some good, out of Bunyan's *Holy War* (which I perversely preferred to *The Pilgrim's Progress*) and Livingstone's *Missionary Journals and Researches*, and a book about the Scotch Covenanters. These volumes shortened many a Sunday. I also liked parts of *The Compleat Angler*, but the best parts I skipped.

"With the coming of school days the time for reading was reduced, and it became necessary to make a choice among books. The natural instincts of youth asserted themselves, and I became a devotee of Captain Mayne Reid and R. M. Ballantyne, whose simple narratives of wild adventure offered a refuge from the mo-

notony of academic life. It gave me no concern that the names of these authors were not
included in the encyclopædias of literature nor
commented upon in the critical reviews. I had
no use for the encyclopædias or reviews; but
*The Young Voyageurs, The White Chief, Osceola
the Seminole, The Bush Boys, The Coral Island,
Red Eric, Ungava,* and *The Gorilla Hunters* gave
me unaffected delight.

"After about two years of this innocent dissi-
pation I began to feel the desire for a better
life, and turned, by my father's advice, to Sir
Walter Scott. *Ivanhoe* and *The Pirate* pleased
me immensely; *Waverley* and *The Heart of Midlothian* I accepted with qualifications; but the
two of Scott's novels that gave me the most
pleasure, I regret to state, were *Quentin Dur-
ward* and *Count Robert of Paris.* Then Dickens
claimed me, and I yielded to the spell of *Oliver
Twist, David Copperfield,* and *Pickwick Papers.*

"By this time it had begun to dawn upon me
that there is a difference among books, not only
in regard to the things told, but also in regard
to the way of the telling. Unconsciously I became sensitive to the magic of style, and, wandering freely through the library, was drawn to
the writers whose manner and accent had a
charm for me. Emerson and Carlyle I liked no

better than I liked caviar; but Lamb's *Essays* and Irving's *Sketches* were fascinating. For histories of literature, thank Heaven, I never had any appetite. I preferred real books to books about books. My only idea of literature was a vivid reflection of life in the world of fancy or in the world of fact.

"In poetry, Milton's *Comus* was about the first thing that took a slight hold of me; I cannot tell why—perhaps it was because I liked my father's reading of it. But even he could not persuade me to anything more than a dim respect for *Paradise Lost*. Some of Shakespeare's plays entranced me; particularly *The Tempest*, *Romeo and Juliet*, and *As You Like It;* but there were others which made no real impression upon my wayward mind. Dryden and Pope and Cowper I tried in vain to appreciate; the best that I could attain to was a distant respect. *The Lady of the Lake* and *The Ancient Mariner*, on the contrary, were read without an effort and with sincere joy. The first book of poetry that I bought for myself was Tennyson's *Enoch Arden*, and I never regretted the purchase, for it led me on, somehow or other, into the poetic studies and the real intimacy with books which enabled me to go through college without serious damage.

"I cannot remember just when I first read *Henry Esmond;* perhaps it was about the beginning of sophomore year. But, at all events, it was then that I ceased to love books as a boy and began to love them as a man."

"And do you still love *Henry Esmond?*" I asked.

"I do indeed," said my Uncle Peter, "and I call it the greatest of English novels. But very close to it I put *David Copperfield, Lorna Doone,* and *The Heart of Midlothian,* and *The Cloister and the Hearth,* and *The Ordeal of Richard Feverel,* and *John Inglesant.*"

"If you love *John Inglesant,*" said I, "you must be getting old, Uncle Peter."

"Oh, no," he answered, comfortably lighting his pipe with a live coal of wood from the hearth, "I am only growing up."

AMONG THE QUANTOCK
HILLS

AMONG THE QUANTOCK HILLS

MY little Dorothea was the only one of the merry party who cared to turn aside with me from the beaten tourist-track, and give up the sight of another English cathedral for the sake of a quiet day among the Quantock Hills. Was it the literary association of that little corner of Somersetshire with the names of Wordsworth and Coleridge that attracted her, I wonder? Or was it the promise that we would hire a dog-cart, if one could be found, and that she should be the driver all through the summer day? I confess my incompetence to decide the question. When one is fifteen years old, a live horse may be as interesting as two dead poets. Not for the world would I put Dorothea to the embarrassment of declaring which was first in her mind.

When she and I got out of the railway carriage, in the early morning, at the humble station of Watchet, (barely mentioned in the guidebook,) our travelling companions jeered gently at our enterprise. As the train rumbled away from the platform, they stuck their heads out of the window and cried, "Where are you going? And how are you going to get there?" Upon my honour, I did not know. That was just the fun of it.

But there was an inn at Watchet, though I doubt whether it had ever entertained tourists. The friendly and surprised landlady thought that she could get us a dog-cart to drive across the country; but it would take about an hour to make ready. So we strolled about the town, and saw the sights of Watchet.

They were few and simple; yet something, (perhaps the generous sunshine of the July day, or perhaps an inward glow of contentment in our hearts,) made them bright and memorable. There were the quaint, narrow streets, with their tiny shops and low stone houses. There was the coast-guard station, with its trim garden, perched on a terrace above the sea. There was the life-boat house, with its doors wide open, and the great boat, spick and span in the glory of new paint, standing ready on its rollers, and the record of splendid rescues in past years inscribed upon the walls. There was the circular basin-harbour, with the workmen slowly repairing the breakwater, and a couple of ancient looking schooners reposing on their sides in the mud at low tide. And there, back on the hill, looking down over the town and far away across the yellow waters of the Bristol Channel, was the high tower of St. Decuman's Church.

"It was from this tiny harbour," said I to Dorothea, "that a great friend of ours, the Ancient Mariner, set sail on a wonderful voyage. Do you remember?

> *'The ship was cheered, the harbour cleared,*
> *Merrily did we drop*
> *Below the kirk, below the hill,*
> *Below the lighthouse top.'*

That was the kirk to which he looked back as he sailed away to an unknown country."

"But, father," said Dorothea, "the Ancient Mariner was not a real person. He was only a character!"

"Are you quite sure," said I, "that a character isn't a real person? At all events, it was here that Coleridge, walking from Nether Stowey to Dulverton, saw the old sailor-man. And since Coleridge saw him, I reckon he lived, and still lives. Are we ever going to forget what he has told us?

> *'He prayeth best, who loveth best*
> *All things both great and small;*
> *For the dear God who loveth us,*
> *He made and loveth all.'"*

Just then a most enchanting little boy and
his sister, not more than five years old, came
sauntering down the gray street, hand in hand.
They were on their way to school, at least an
hour late, round and rosy, careless and merry,
manifest owners of the universe. We stopped
them: they were dismayed, but resolute. We
gave each of them a penny; they radiated wonder and joy. Too happy for walking, they
skipped and toddled on their way, telling everyone they met, children and grown-up people, of
the good fortune that had befallen them. We
could see them far down the street, pausing a
moment to look in at the shop-windows, or
holding up their coppers while they stopped
some casual passer-by and made him listen to
their story—just like the Ancient Mariner.

By this time the dog-cart was ready. The
landlord charged me eighteen shillings for the
drive to Bridgewater, nineteen miles away, stop-
ping where we liked, and sending back the cart
with the post-boy that evening. By the look
on his face I judged that he thought it was too
much. But I did not. So we climbed to the
high seat, Dorothea took the reins and the whip,
and we set forth for a day of unguide-booked
pleasure.

What good roads they have in England!
Look at the piles of broken stone for repairs,

stored in little niches all along the way; see how promptly and carefully every hole is filled up and every break mended; and you will understand how a small beast can pull a heavy load in this country, and why the big draught-horses wear long and do good work. A country with a fine system of roads is like a man with a good circulation of the blood; the labour of life becomes easier, effort is reduced and pleasure increased.

Bowling along the smooth road we crossed a small river at Doniford, where a man was wading the stream below the bridge and fly-fishing for trout; we passed the farmhouses of Rydon, where the steam-thresher was whirling, and the wheat was falling in golden heaps, and the pale-yellow straw was mounded in gigantic ricks; and then we climbed the hill behind St. Audries, with its pretty gray church, and manor house half hidden in the great trees of the park.

The view was one of indescribable beauty and charm; soft, tranquil woods and placid fertile fields; thatched cottages here and there, sheltered and embowered in green; far away on the shore, the village of East Quantockshead; beyond that the broad, tossing waters of the Bristol Channel; and beyond that again, thirty miles away, the silver coast of Wales and the blue mountains fading into the sky. Ships were sailing in and out, toy-like in the distance. Far to the north-west, we could see the cliffs of the Devonshire coast; to the north-east the islands of Steep Holm and Flat Holm rose from the Severn Sea; and around the point beyond them, in the little churchyard of Clevedon, I knew that the dust of Arthur Henry Hallam, whose friendship Tennyson has immortalized in *In Memoriam*, was sleeping

" By the pleasant shore
And in hearing of the wave."

High overhead the great white clouds were loitering across the deep-blue heaven. White butterflies wavered above the road. Tall foxglove spires lit the woodland shadows with rosy gleams. Bluebells and golden ragwort fringed the hedge-rows. A family of young wrens fluttered in and out of the hawthorns. A yellowhammer, with cap of gold, warbled his sweet, common little song. The colour of the earth was warm and red; the grass was of a green so vivid that it seemed to be full of conscious gladness. It was a day and a scene to calm and satisfy the heart.

At Kilve, a straggling village along the roadside, I remembered Wordsworth's poem called *An Anecdote for Fathers*. The little boy in the poem says that he would rather be at Kilve

than at Liswyn. When his father foolishly
presses him to give a reason for his preference,
he invents one:

> "*At Kilve there was no weather-cock,*
> *And that's the reason why.*"

Naturally, I looked around the village to see
whether it would still answer to the little boy's
description. Sure enough, there was no weather-
cock in sight, not even on the church-tower.

Not far beyond Kilve we saw a white house,
a mile or so away, standing among the trees to
the south, at the foot of the high-rolling Quantock Hills. Our post-boy told us that it was
Alfoxton, "where Muster Wudswuth used to
live," but just how to get to it he did not know.
So we drove into the next village of Holford and
made inquiry at the "Giles' Plough Inn," a
most quaint and rustic tavern with a huge
ancient sign-board on the wall, representing
Giles with his white horse and his brown horse
and his plough. Turning right and left and
right again, through narrow lanes, between cottages gay with flowers, we came to a wicket-
gate beside an old stone building, and above
the gate a notice warning all persons not to
trespass on the grounds of Alfoxton. But the
gate was on the latch, and a cottager, passing
by, told us that there was a "right of way"

which could not be closed—"goä straight on,
and nivver feär, nubbody 'll harm ye."

A few steps brought us into the thick woods
and to the edge of a deep glen, spanned by a
bridge made of a single long tree-trunk, with a
hand-rail at one side. Down below us, as we
stood on the swaying bridge, a stream dashed
and danced and sang through the shade, among
the ferns and mosses and wild flowers. The
steep sides of the glen glistened with hollies and
laurels, tangled and confused with blackberry
bushes. Overhead was the interwoven roof of
oaks and ashes and beeches. Here it was that
Wordsworth, in the year 1797, when he was
feeling his way back from the despair of mind
which followed the shipwreck of his early revolutionary dreams, used to wander alone or with
his dear sister Dorothy. And here he composed
the *Lines Written in Early Spring*—almost the
first notes of his new poetic power:

> "*I heard a thousand blended notes,*
>   *While in a grove I sat reclined,*
>   *In that sweet mood when pleasant thoughts*
>   *Bring sad thoughts to the mind.*

> "*Through primrose tufts, in that green bower,*
>   *The periwinkle trailed its leaves;*
>   *And 'tis my faith that every flower*
>   *Enjoys the air it breathes.*"

AMONG THE QUANTOCK HILLS

Climbing up to the drive, we followed a long curving avenue toward the house. It led along the breast of the hill, with a fine view under the spreading arms of the great beeches, across the water to the Welsh mountains. On the left the woods were thick. Huge old hollies showed the ravages of age and storm. A riotous undergrowth of bushes and bracken filled the spaces between the taller trees. Doves were murmuring in the shade. Rabbits scampered across the road. In an open park at the edge of the wood, a herd of twenty or thirty fallow deer with pale spotted sides and twinkling tails trotted slowly up the slope.

Alfoxton House is a long, two-story building of white stucco, with a pillared porch facing the hills. The back looks out over a walled garden, with velvet turf and brilliant flowers and pretty evergreens, toward the sea-shore. The house has been much changed and enlarged since the days when young William Wordsworth rented it, (hardly more than a good farmhouse), for twenty-three pounds a year, and lived in it with his sister from 1797 to 1798, in order to be near his friend Coleridge at Nether Stowey. There is not a room that remains the same, though the present owner has wisely brought together as much of the old wood-work as possible into one chamber, which is known as Wordsworth's

study. But the poet's real study was out of
doors; and it was there that we looked for the
things that he loved.

In a field beyond the house there were two
splendid old ash-trees, which must have been
full-grown in Wordsworth's day. We stretched
ourselves among the gnarled roots, my little
Dorothy and I, and fed our eyes upon the view
that must have often refreshed him, while his
Dorothy was leading his heart back with gentle
touches toward the recovery of joy. There was
the soft, dimpled landscape, in tones of silvery
verdure, blue in distance, green near at hand,
sloping down to the shining sea. The sky was
delicate and friendly, bending close above us,
with long lines of snowy clouds. There was
hardly a breath of wind. Far to the east we
saw the rich plain rolling away to Bridgewater
and the bare line of the distant Mendip Hills.
Shadows of clouds swept slowly across the land.
Colours shifted and blended. On the steep
hill behind us a row of trees stood out clear
against the blue.

"With ships the sea was sprinkled far and nigh."

What induced Wordsworth to leave a place
so beautiful? A most prosaic reason. He was
practically driven out by the suspicion and mis-

trust of his country neighbours. A poet was a creature that they could not understand. His long rambles among the hills by day and night, regardless of the weather; his habit of talking to himself; his intimacy and his constant conferences on unknown subjects with Coleridge, whose radical ideas were no secret; his friendship with Thelwall the republican, who came to reside in the neighbourhood; the rumour that the poet had lived in France and sympathized with the Revolution—all these were dark and damning evidences to the rustic mind that there was something wrong about this long-legged, sober-faced, feckless young man. Probably he was a conspirator, plotting the overthrow of the English Government, or at least of the Tory party. So ran the talk of the country-side; and the lady who owned Alfoxton was so alarmed by it that she declined to harbour such a dangerous tenant any longer. Wordsworth went with his sister to Germany in 1798; and in the following year they found a new home at Dove Cottage, by Grasmere, among the English lakes.

On our way out to the place where we had left our equipage, we met the owner of the estate, walking with his dogs. He was much less fierce than his placard. It may have been something in Dorothea's way that mollified him, but at all events he turned and walked with us to show us the way up the "Hareknap"—the war-path of ancient armies—to a famous point of view. There we saw the Quantock Hills, rolling all around us. They were like long smooth steep billows of earth, covered with bracken, and gorse, and heather just coming into bloom. Thick woodlands hung on their sides, but above their purple shoulders the ridges were bare. They looked more than a thousand feet high. Among their cloven combes, deep-thicketed and watered with cool springs, the wild red deer still find a home. And it was here (not in Cardiganshire as the poem puts it) that Wordsworth's old huntsman, "Simon Lee," followed the chase of the stag.

It was a three-mile drive from Holford to Nether Stowey. Dorothea remarked that Coleridge and the Wordsworths must have been great walkers if this was their idea of living close together. And so they were, for that bit of road seemed to them only a prelude to a real walk of twenty or thirty miles. The exercise put them in tune for poetry, and their best thoughts came to them when they were afoot.

"The George" at Nether Stowey is a very modest inn, the entrance paved with flag-stones, the only public room a low-ceiled parlour; but its merits are far beyond its pretensions. We lunched there most comfortably on roast duck and green peas, cherry tart and cheese, and then set out to explore the village, which is closely built along the roads whose junction is marked by a little clock-tower. The market-street is paved with cobble-stones, and down one side of it runs a small brook, partly built in and covered over, but making a merry noise all the way. Coleridge speaks of it in his letters as "the dear gutter of Stowey."

Just outside of the town is the Castle Mound, a steep, grassy hill, to the top of which we climbed. There was the distinct outline of the foundations of the old castle, built in the Norman times; we could trace the moat, and the court, and all the separate rooms; but not a stone of the walls remained—only a ground-plan drawn in the turf of the hill-top. All the pride and power of the Norman barons had passed like the clouds that were sailing over the smooth ridges of the Quantocks.

Coleridge was twenty-four years old when he came to Nether Stowey with his young wife and a boy baby. Troubles had begun to gather around him; he was very poor, tormented with neuralgia, unable to find regular occupation, and estranged by a quarrel from his friend and brother-in-law, Robert Southey. Thomas Poole, a well-to-do tanner at Nether Stowey, a man of good education and high character, a great lover of poetry and liberty, had befriended Coleridge and won his deep regard and affection. Nothing would do but that Poole should find a cottage near to his own house, where the poet could live in quietude and congenial companionship.

The cottage was found; and, in spite of Poole's misgivings about its size, and his warnings in regard to the tedium and depression of village life, Coleridge took it and moved in with his little family on the last day of the year 1796—a cold season for a "flitting!" We can imagine the young people coming down the Bridgewater road through the wintry weather with their few household goods in a cart.

The cottage was at the western end of the village; and there it stands yet, a poor, ugly house, close on the street. We went in, and after making clear to the good woman who owned it that we were not looking for lodgings, we saw all that there was to see of the dwelling. There were four rooms, two downstairs and two above. All were bare and disorderly, because, as the woman explained, house-cleaning was in progress. It was needed. She showed us a winding stair, hardly better than a ladder, which led from the lower to the upper rooms. There was no view, no garden. But in Coleridge's day there was a small plot of ground belonging to the house and running back to the large and pleasant place of his friend Poole. It was upon this little garden that the imagination of the new tenant was fixed, and there he saw, in his dream, the corn and the cabbages and the potatoes growing luxuriantly under his watchful and happy care; enough, he hoped, to feed himself and his family, and to keep a couple of what he called "snouted and grunting cousins" on the surplus. "Literature," he wrote, "though I shall never abandon it, will always be a secondary object with me. My poetic vanity and my political favour have been exhaled, and I would rather be an expert, self-maintaining gardener than a Milton, if I could not unite them both." How amusing are men's dreams—those of humility as well as those of ambition! There is a peculiarly Coleridgean touch in that last hint of uniting Milton and the market-gardener.

In fact, I doubt whether the garden ever paid expenses; but, on the other hand, the crop of poetry that sprung from Coleridge's marvellous mind was rich and splendid. It was while he lived in this poor little cottage that he produced *Osorio, Fears in Solitude, Ode to France,* the first part of *Christabel, Frost at Midnight, The Nightingale, Kubla Khan,* and *The Ancient Mariner,* and planned with his friend Wordsworth *Lyrical Ballads,* the most epoch-making book of modern English poetry. Truly this year, from April, 1797, to April, 1798, was the *annus mirabilis* of his life. Never again was he so happy, never again did he do such good work, as when he harboured in this cottage, and slipped through the back gate to walk in the garden or read in the library of his good friend, Thomas Poole, or trudged down the road to the woods of Alfoxton to talk with the Wordsworths. He wrote lovingly of the place:

"*And now, beloved Stowey, I behold*
  Thy Church-tower, and methinks, the four huge elms
  Clustering, which mark the mansion of my friend;
  And close behind them, hidden from my view,
  Is my own lovely cottage, where my babe
  And my babe's mother dwell in peace."

Dorothea and I were not sure that Mrs. Coleridge enjoyed the cottage as much as he did. Greta Hall, Southey's house, at Keswick, with its light airy rooms and its splendid view, was her next home; and when we saw it, a few weeks later, we were glad that the babe and the babe's mother had lived there.

But the afternoon was waning, and we must turn our back to the Quantocks, and take the road again. Past the church and the manor house, with its odd little turreted summer-house, or *gazébo*, perched on the corner of the garden-wall; past a row of ancient larch-trees and a grove of Scotch pines; past smooth-rolling meadows full of cattle and sheep; past green orchards full of fruit for the famous and potent Somerset cider; past the old town of Cannington, where the fair Rosamund was born, and where, on our day, we saw the whole population in the streets, perturbed by some unknown excitement and running to and fro like mad folks; past sleepy farms and spacious parks and snug villas, we rolled along the high-road, into Bridgewater, a small city, where they make "Bath bricks," and where the statue of Admiral Blake swaggers sturdily in the market-place. There we took the train to join our friends at dinner in Bristol; and so ended our day among the Quantock Hills.

BETWEEN THE LUPIN AND THE LAUREL

BETWEEN THE LUPIN AND
THE LAUREL

NO other time of the year, on our northern
Atlantic seaboard, is so alluring, so delicate
and subtle in its charm, as that which follows
the fading of the bright blue lupins in the meadows and along the banks of the open streams,
and precedes the rosy flush of myriad laurels in
full bloom on the half-wooded hillsides, and in
the forest glades, and under the lofty shadow of
the groves of yellow pine. Then, for a little
while, the spring delays to bourgeon into summer: the woodland maid lingers at the garden
gate of womanhood, reluctant to enter and leave
behind the wild sweetness of freedom and un-
certainty.

Winter is gone for good and all. There is no
fear that he will come sneaking back with cold
hands to fetch something that he has forgotten.
Nature is secure of another season of love, of
mating, of germination, of growth, of maturity
—a fair four months in which the joyful spirit
of life may have its way and work its will. The
brown earth seems to thrill and quicken every-

where with new impulses which transform it into springing grass and overflowing flowers. The rivers are at their best: strong and clear and musical, the turbulence of early floods departed, the languor of later droughts not yet appearing. The shrunken woods expand; the stringent, sparkling wintry stars grow mild and liquid, shining with a tremulous and tender light; the whole world seems larger, happier, more full of untold, untried possibilities. The air vibrates with wordless promises, calls, messages, beckonings; and fairy-tales are told by all the whispering leaves.

Yet though the open season is now secure, it is not yet settled. No chance of a relapse into the winter, but plenty of change in the unfolding of the summer. There are still caprices and wayward turns in nature's moods; cold nights when the frost-elves are hovering in the upper air; windy mornings which shake and buffet the tree-tassels and light embroidered leaves; sudden heats of tranquil noon through which the sunlight pours like a flood of eager love, pressing to create new life.

Birds are still mating; and quarrelling, too. Their songs, their cries of agitation and expectancy, their call notes, their lyrical outpourings of desire are more varied and more copious than

128

ever. All day long they are singing, and every hour on the wing, coming up from the southward, passing on to the northward, fluttering through the thickets, exploring secret places, choosing homes and building nests. In every coppice there is a running to and fro, a creeping, a scampering, and a leaping of wild creatures. At the roots of the bushes and weeds and sedges, in the soft recesses of the moss, and through the intricate tangle of withered grass-blades pierced with bright-green shoots, there is a manifold stir of insect life. In the air millions of gauzy wings are quivering, swarms of ethereal, perishable creatures rising and falling and circling in mystical dances of joy. Fish are leaping along the stream. The night breeze trembles with the shrill, piercing chorus of the innumerable hylas.

Late trees, like the ash, the white oak, the butternut, are still delaying to put forth their full foliage; veiled in tender, transparent green, or flushed with faint pink, they stand as if they were waiting for a set time; and the tiny round buds on the laurels, clustered in countless umbels of bright rose among the dark green glistening leaves, are closed, hiding their perfect beauty until the day appointed. It is the season of the unfulfilled desire, the eager hope, the coming surprise. To-day the world is beautiful; but to-morrow, next day—who knows when?—something more beautiful is coming, something new, something perfect. This is the charm of wild nature between the lupin and the laurel.

At such a season it is hard to stay at home. The streets all seem to lead into the country, and one longs to follow their leading, out into the highway, on into the winding lane, on into the wood-road, on and on, until one comes to that mysterious and delightful ending, (told of in the familiar saying,) where the road finally dwindles into a squirrel track and runs up a tree—not an ending at all, you see, but really a beginning! For there is the tree; and if you climb it, who knows what new landscape, what lively adventure, will open before you? At any rate, you will get away from the tyranny of the commonplace, the conventional, the methodical, which transforms the rhythm of life into a logarithm. Even a small variation, a taste of surprise, will give you what you need as a spring tonic: the sense of escape, a day off.

Living in a university town, and participating with fidelity in its principal industry, I find that my own particular nightmare of monotony takes the form of examination papers—quires of them, reams of them, stacks of them—a horrid

incubus, always oppressive, but then most un-
endurable when the book-room begins to smell
musty in the morning, and the fire is unlit upon
the hearth, and last night's student-lamp is
stuck all over with tiny dead gnats, and the
breath of the blossoming grape is wafted in at
the open window, and the robins, those melo-
dious rowdies, are whistling and piping over the
lawn and through the trees in voluble mockery
of the professor's task. "Come out," they say,
"come out! Why do you look in a book?
Double, double, toil and trouble! Give it up—
tup, tup, tup! Come away and play for a day.
What do you know? Let it go. You're as dry
as a chip, chip, chip! Come out, won't you?
will you?"

Truly, these examination questions that I
framed with such pains look very dull and
tedious now—a desiccation of the beautiful
work of the great poets. And these answers
that the boys have wrought out with such pains,
on innumerable pads of sleazy white paper, how
little they tell me of what the fellows really
know and feel! Examination papers are "requisite and necessary," of course; I can't deny it—
requisite formalities and necessary absurdities.
But to turn the last page of the last pad, and
mark it with a red pencil and add it to the pile

of miseries past, and slip away from books to nature, from learning to life, between the lupin and the laurel—that is a pleasure doubled by release from pain.

I think a prize should be offered for the discovery of good places to take a free and natural outing within easy reach of the great city and the routine of civilized work—just-over-the-fence retreats, to which you can run off without much preparation, and from which you can come back again before your little world discovers your absence. That was the charm of Hopkinson Smith's sketch, *A Day at Laguerre's;* and an English writer who calls himself "A Son of the Marshes" has written a delightful book of interviews with birds and other wild things, which bears the attractive title, *Within an Hour of London Town.* But I would make it a condition of the prize that the name of the hiding-place should not be published, lest the careless, fad-following crowd should flock thither and spoil it. Let the precious news be communicated only by word of mouth, or by letter, as a confidence and gift of friendship, so that none but the like-minded may strike the trail to the next-door remnant of Eden.

It was thus that my four friends—Friends in creed as well as in deed—told to me, one of

THE LUPIN AND THE LAUREL

"the world's people," toiling over my benumbing examination papers, their secret find of a little river in South Jersey, less than an hour from Philadelphia, where one could float in a canoe through mile after mile of unbroken woodland, and camp at night in a bit of wilderness as wildly fair as when the wigwams of the Lenni-Lenape were hidden among its pine groves. The Friends said that they "had a concern" to guide me to their delectable retreat, and that they hoped the "way would open" for me to come. Canoes and tents and camp-kit? "That will all be provided; it is well not to be anxious concerning these sublunary things." Mosquitoes? "Concerning this, also, thee must learn to put thy trust in Providence; yet there is a happy interval, as it were, between the fading of the hepatica and the blooming of the mosquito, when the woods of South Jersey are habitable for man, and it would be most prudent to choose this season for the exercise of providential trust regarding mosquitoes." Examination papers? Duty? "Surely thee must do what thee thinks will do most good, and follow the inward voice. And if it calls thee to stay with the examination papers, or if it calls thee to go with us, whichever way, thee will be resigned to obey." Fortunately, there was no

133

doubt about the inward voice; it was echoing the robins; it was calling me to go out like Elijah and dwell under a juniper-tree. I replied to the Friends in the words of one of their own preachers: "I am resigned to go, or resigned to stay, but most resigned to go"; and we went.

The statue of William Penn seemed to look benignantly down upon us as we passed, bag and bundle in hand, along the regular Philadelphia short-cut which leads through the bowels of the Court-house, from the Broad Street railway station to John Wanamaker's store. Philadelphians always have the air of doing something very modern, hurried, and time-saving when they lead you through that short-cut. But we were not really in a hurry; we had all the time there is; we could afford to gape a little in the shop-windows. The spasmodic Market Street trolley-car and the deliberate Camden ferry-boat were rapid enough for us. The gait of the train on the Great Sandy and Oceanic Railway was neither too fast nor too slow. Even the deserted condition of Hummingtown, where we disembarked about eleven o'clock in the morning, and found that the entire population had apparently gone to a Decoration Day ball-game, leaving post-office, telegraph station, fruit store, bakery, all closed—

even this failure to meet our expectations did not put us out of humour with the universe, or call forth rude words on the degeneracy of modern times.

Our good temper was imperturbable; for had we not all "escaped as a bird from the hand of the fowler"—Master Thomas from the mastery of his famous boarding-school in Old Chester, and Friends Walter and Arthur from the uninspired scripture of their ledgers and day-books, and I from the incubation of those hideous examination papers, and the gentle Friend William from his—there! I have forgotten what particular monotony William was glad to get away from; but I know it was from something. I could read it in his face; in his pleased, communicative silence; in the air of almost reckless abandon with which he took off his straight-breasted Quaker coat, and started out in his shirt-sleeves to walk with Walter, ahead of the cart which carried our two canoes and the rest of us over to the river.

It was just an ordinary express wagon, with two long, heavy planks fastened across the top of it. On these the canoes were lashed, with their prows projecting on either flank of the huge, pachydermatous horse, who turned his head slowly from one side to the other, as he stalked along the level road, and looked back at his new environment with stolid wonder. He must have felt as if he were suffering "a sea change," and going into training for Neptune's stud. The driver sat on the dashboard between the canoes; and Master Thomas, Arthur, and I were perched upon the ends of the planks with our feet dangling over the road. It was not exactly what one would call an elegant equipage, but it rolled along.

The road was of an uncompromising straightness. It lay across the slightly undulating sandy plain like a long yellow ruler; and on each side were the neatly marked squares and parallelograms of the little truck farms, all cultivated by Italians. Their new and unabashed frame houses were freshly painted in incredible tones of carrot yellow, pea green, and radish red. The few shade trees and the many fruit trees, with whitewashed trunks, were set out in unbending regularity of line. The women and children were working in the rows of strawberries which covered acre after acre of white sand with stripes of deep green. Some groups of people by the wayside were chattering merrily together in the language which Byron calls

" That soft bastard Latin
Which melts like kisses from a woman's mouth."

THE LUPIN AND THE LAUREL

It was a scene of foreign industry and cheerfulness, a bit of little Italy transplanted. Only the landscape was distinctly not Italian, but South Jersey to the core. Yet the people seemed at home and happy in it. Perhaps prosperity made up to them for the loss of picturesqueness.

At New Prussia the road was lifted by a little ridge, and for a few minutes we travelled through another European country. Two young men were passing ball in front of a beer saloon. "Vot's der news?" said one of them in a strong German accent. We were at a loss for an answer, as it was rather a dull time in international politics; but Master Thomas began to say something about the riots in Russia. "Russia hell!" said the young man. "How's der ball-game? Vas our nine or Hummingtown ahead yet?" We could give no information on this important subject, but we perceived that New Prussia was already Americanized.

A mile or so beyond this the road dipped gently into a shallow, sparsely wooded valley and we came to a well-built stone bridge which spanned, with a single narrow arch, the little river of our voyage. It was like a big brook, flowing with deep, brown current out of a thicket, and on through a small cranberry bog below the bridge. Here we launched and loaded our canoes, and went down with the stream, through a bit of brushy woodland, till we found a good place for luncheon. For though it was long past noon and we were very hungry, we wanted to get really into the woods before we broke bread together.

Scanty woods they were, indeed; just a few scrub pines growing out of a bank of clean white sand. But we spread a rubber blanket in their thin shade, and set forth our repast of biscuits and smoked beef and olives, and fell to eating as heartily and merrily as if it had been a banquet. The yellow warblers and the song sparrows were flitting about us; and two cat-birds and a yellow-throat were singing from the thicket on the opposite shore. There were patches of snowy sand-myrtle and yellow pov-erty-plant growing around our table; tiny, hardy, heath-like creatures, delicately wrought with bloom as if for a king's palace; irrepressible and lovely offspring of the yearning for beauty that hides in the poorest place of earth. In a still arm of the stream, a few yards above us, was a clump of the long, naked flower-scapes of the golden-club, now half entered upon their silvery stage.

It was strange what pleasure these small gifts of blossom and song brought to us. We were in the mood which Wordsworth describes in the lines written in his pocket-copy of *The Castle of Indolence*:

"There did they dwell, from earthly labour free,
  As happy spirits as were ever seen;
If but a bird, to keep them company,
  Or butterfly sate down, they were, I ween,
    As pleased as if the same had been a Maiden-
      queen."

But our "earthly labour" began again when we started down the stream; for now we had fairly entered the long strip of wilderness which curtains its winding course. On either hand the thickets came down so close to the water that there were no banks left; just woods and water blending; and the dark topaz current swirling and gurgling through a clump of bushes or round the trunk of a tree, as if it did not care what path it took so long as it got through. Alders and pussy-willows, viburnums, clethras, choke-cherries, swamp maples, red birches, and all sorts of trees and shrubs that are water-loving, made an intricate labyrinth for the stream to thread; and through the tangle, cat-briers, blackberries, fox grapes, and poison ivy were interlaced.

Worst of all was the poison ivy, which seemed

139

here to deserve its other name of poison oak,
for it was more like a tree than a vine, flinging
its knotted branches from shore to shore, and
thrusting its pallid, venomous blossoms into our
faces. Walter was especially susceptible to the
influence of this poison, so we put him in the
middle of our canoe, and I, being a veteran and
immune, took the bow-paddle. It was no easy
task to guide the boat down the swift current,
for it was bewilderingly crooked, twisting and
turning upon itself in a way that would have
made the far-famed Mæander look like a straight
line. Many a time it ran us deep into the
alders, or through a snarl of thorn-set vines, or
crowded us under the trunk of an overhanging
tree. We glimpsed the sun through the young
leaves, now on our right hand, now on our left,
now in front of us, and now over our shoulders.
After several miles of this curliewurlie course,
the incoming of the Penny Pot Stream on the
left broadened the flowing trail a little. Not
far below that, the Hospitality Branch poured
in its abundant waters on the right, and we
went floating easily down a fair, open river.

There were banks now, and they were fringed
with green borders of aquatic plants, rushes,
and broad spatter-docks, and flags, and arrowheads, and marsh-marigolds, and round-leaved

140

pond-lilies, and pointed pickerel-weed. The current was still rapid and strong, but it flowed smoothly through the straight reaches and around the wide curves. On either hand the trees grew taller and more stately. The mellow light of afternoon deepened behind them, and the rich cloud colours of approaching sunset tinged the mirror of the river with orange and rose. We floated into a strip of forest. The stream slackened and spread out, broadening into the head of a pond. On the left, there was a point of higher land, almost like a low bluff, rising ten or twelve feet above the water and covered with a grove of oaks and white pines. Here we beached our canoes and made our first camp.

A slender pole was nailed horizontally between two trees, and from this the shelter tent was stretched with its sloping roof to the breeze and its front open toward the pond. There were no balsam or hemlock boughs for the beds, so we gathered armfuls of fallen leaves and pine needles, and spread our blankets on this rude mattress. Arthur and Walter cut wood for the fire. Master Thomas and William busied themselves with the supper. There was a famous dish of scrambled eggs, and creamed potatoes, and bacon, and I know not what else. We ate

141

till we could eat no more, and then we sat in the wide-open tent, with the camp-fire blazing in front of us, and talked of everything under the stars.

I like the Quaker speech: the gentle intimacy of their "little language," with its quaint "thees" and "thous," and the curious turn they give to their verbs, disregarding the formalities of grammar. "Will thee go," "has thee seen," "does thee like"—that is the way they speak it; an unjustifiable way, I know, but it sounds pleasant. I like the Quaker spirit and manners, at least as I have found them in my friends: sober but not sad, plain but very considerate, genuinely simple in the very texture of their thoughts and feelings, and not averse to that quiet mirth which leaves no bitter taste behind it. One thing that I cannot understand in Charles Lamb is his confession, in the essay on *Imperfect Sympathies*, that he had a prejudice against Quakers. But then I remember that one of his best bits of prose is called *A Quaker's Meeting*, and one of his best poems is about the Quaker maiden, Hester Savory, and one of his best lovers and companions was the broad-brim Bernard Barton. I conclude that there must be different kinds of Quakers as there are of other folks, and that my particular Friends belong to the tribe of Bernard and Hester, and their spiritual ancestry is in the same line with the poet Whittier.

Yet even these four are by no means of one pattern. William is the youngest of the group, but the oldest-fashioned Friend, still clinging very closely to the old doctrines and the old ritual of silent simplicity, and wearing the straight-cut, collarless coat, above which his youthful face looks strangely ascetic and serene. I can imagine him taking joyfully any amount of persecution for his faith, in the ancient days; but in these tolerant modern times, he has the air of waiting very tranquilly and with good humour for the world to see that the old ways are the best, and to come round to them again.

Walter and Arthur are Young Quakers, men of their time, diligent in business, fond of music and poetry, loyal to the society of their fathers, but more than willing to see its outward manners and customs, and even some of its ways of teaching, quietly modified to meet the needs and conditions of the present. In appearance you could hardly tell them from the world's people; yet I perceive that inwardly the meeting-house has made its indelible mark upon them in a certain poise of mind and restraint of temper, a sweet assurance of unseen things, and a mind expectant of spiritual visitations.

Master Thomas, the leader of our expedition, is a veteran school-teacher, in one of the largest and most successful of the Friends' boarding-schools. To him I think there is neither old nor new in doctrine; there is only the truth, and the only way to be sure of it is by living. He is a fervent instructor, to whom an indifferent scholar is a fascinating problem, and a pupil who "cannot understand mathematics" offers a new adventure. But part of his instruction, and the part to which he gives himself most ardently, is the knowledge and love of the great out-of-doors. Every summer he runs a guest-camp in the Adirondacks, and in the fall he gives a big camp-supper for the old pupils of his school, who come back by the hundred to renew their comradeship with "Master Thomas." It is good to have an academic title like that. Arthur and William and Walter are among his old boys, and they still call him by that name. But it is partly because he has also been their master in fire-making, and tent-pitching, and cooking, and canoe-building, and other useful arts which are not in the curriculum of book-learning.

Here, then, I have sketched the friends who

sat with me before the glowing logs on that cool, starry night, within a few miles of the railroad and not far away from the roaring town, yet infinitely deep in the quietude of nature's heart. Of the talk I can remember little, except that it was free and friendly, natural and good. But one or two stories that they told me of a famous old Philadelphia Quaker, Nicholas Waln, have stuck in my memory.

His piety was tempered with a strong sense of humour, and on one occasion when he was visiting a despondent sister, he was much put out by her plaintive assertions that she was going to die. "I have no doubt," said he finally, "but that thee will; and when thee gets to heaven give my love to the Apostle Paul, and tell him I wish he would come back to earth and explain some of the hard things in his epistles." At another time he overtook a young woman Friend in worldly dress, upon which he remarked, "Satin without, and Satan within." But this time he got as good as he gave, for the young woman added, "And old Nick behind!" When it was the fashion to wear a number of capes, one above another, on a great-coat, Nicholas met a young acquaintance dressed in the mode. Taking hold of one of the capes, the old Quaker asked innocently what it was. "That is Cape Hatteras," said the pert youth. "And this?" said Nicholas, touching another. "Oh, that is Cape Henlopen," was the answer. "Then, I suppose," said Nicholas gravely, pointing to the young man's head, "this must be the lighthouse." I think that Charles Lamb, despite his imperfect sympathy with Quakers, would have liked this turn to the conversation.

Bedtime comes at last, even when you are lodging at the Sign of the Beautiful Star. There were a few quiet words read from a peace-giving book, and a few minutes of silent thought in fellowship, and then each man pulled his blanket round him and slept as if there were no troubles in the world.

Certainly there were none waiting for us in the morning; for the day rose fresh and fair, and we had nothing to do but enjoy it. After fishing for an hour or two, to supply our larder, we paddled down the pond, which presently widened into quite a lake, ending in a long, low dam with trees growing all across it. Here was the forgotten village of Watermouth, founded before the Revolution, and once the seat of a flourishing iron industry, but now stranded between two railways, six miles on either side of it, and basking on the warm sand-hills in a painless and innocent decay.

THE LUPIN AND THE LAUREL

Watermouth had done nothing to deserve ill fortune. But the timber which had once been floated down its river was all cut and gone; and the bog-iron which had once been smelted in its furnaces was all used up; and the forest glass-makers and charcoal-burners who had once traded in its store had all disappeared; and the new colonies of fruit-growers and truck-farmers from Italy and Germany did not like to settle quite so far from the railway; and there was nothing left for Watermouth but to sit in the sun and doze, while one family after another melted away, and house after house closed its windows and its doors.

The manor-house stood in spacious grounds sloping gently down to the southern shore of the lake, well planted with a variety of shade trees and foreign evergreens, but overgrown with long grass and straggling weeds. Master Thomas and I landed, and strolled through the neglected lawn toward the house, in search of a possible opportunity to buy some fresh eggs. The long, pillared veranda, with its French windows opening to the floor; the wide double door giving entrance to a central hall; a score of slight and indefinable signs told us that the mansion had seen its days of comfort and elegance. But there were other signs—a pillar leaning out of plumb, a bit of railing sagging down, a board loose at the corner—which seemed to speak of the pluperfect tense. In a fragment of garden at one side, where a broken trellis led to an arbor more than half hidden by vines, we saw a lady, clad in black, walking slowly among the bewildered roses and clumps of hemerocallis, stooping now and then to pluck a flower or tenderly to lift and put aside a straggling branch.

"This is plainly the mistress of the house," said Master Thomas; "does thee think that we could make bold to speak with her upon the subject of fresh eggs?"

"I think," said I, "that with thy friendly tact thee could speak with anybody upon any subject."

"But my coat?" said Master Thomas, for he had left it in the boat.

"'Tis a warm day, Master Thomas," I answered, "and doubtless the lady will know that thee has a coat, when she hears thee speak. But in any event, it is wise not to think too much of these mundane things. Let us go up."

So we made our salutations, stated our names and our occupations, and described the voyage which had brought us to Watermouth, in a way that led naturally to an explanation of our present need and desire for fresh eggs: though indeed it was hardly necessary to be explicit on that point, for our little tin pail betrayed us as foragers. The lady in black received us with gracious dignity, identified and placed us without difficulty (indeed she knew some relation of each of us), and gave us hospitable assurance that our wants in the matter of eggs could easily be satisfied. Meantime we must come up to the house with her and rest ourselves.

Rest was not an imperative necessity for us just then, but we were glad to see the interior of the old mansion. There was the long drawing-room, with its family portraits running back into the eighteenth century—one of them an admirable painting by Sully—and the library, with its tall book-shelves, now empty, and engravings and autographs hanging on the walls. The lady in black was rather sad; for her father, a distinguished publicist and man of letters, had built this house; and her grandfather, a great iron-master, had owned most of the land hereabouts; and the roots and tendrils of her memory were all entwined about the place; but now she was dismantling it and closing it up, preparatory to going away, perhaps to selling it.

By this time the tin pail had come in, filled with the nutritious fruit of the industrious and faithful hen. So we said farewell to the lady in black, with suitable recognition of her courtesy and kindness, and not without some silent reflections on the mutability of human affairs. Here had been a fine estate, a great family, a prosperous industry firmly established, now fading away like smoke. But I do not believe the lady in black will ever disappear entirely from Watermouth while she lives; for is there not the old meeting-house, a hundred years old (with the bees' nest in the weather-boarding), for her to watch over, and care for, and worship in?

The young men were waiting for us below the dam. Here was a splendid water-power running away almost idle. For the great iron forge, with its massive stone buildings, standing (if the local tradition is correct) on the site where the first American cannon-balls had been cast for the Revolutionary War, and where that shrewd Rhode Islander, Gen. Nathanael Greene, had invested some of the money he made in army contracts, had been put out of business many years ago by the development of iron-making in North Jersey and Pennsylvania. An attempt was made to turn it into a wood-pulp factory; but that had failed because the refractory yellow pine was full of hard knots that refused to let themselves be ground into pulp.

THE LUPIN AND THE LAUREL

Now a feeble little saw-mill was running from time to time in one corner of the huge edifice; and the greater part of the river out of work was foaming and roaring in wasteful beauty over the gates of the dam.

It was here, on the slopes of the open fields and on the dry sides of the long embankment, that we saw the faded remnants of the beauty with which the lupins had surrounded Watermouth a few days before. The innumerable plants with their delicate palmate leaves were still fresh and vigorous; no drought can wither them even in the dryest soil, for their roots reach down to the hidden waters. But their winged blossoms, with which a little while since they had "blued the earth," as Thoreau says, were now almost all gone; as if a countless flock of blue butterflies had taken flight and vanished. Only here and there one could see little groups of belated flowers, scraps of the cœrulean colour, like patches of deep-blue sky seen through the rents in a drifting veil of clouds.

But the river called us away from the remembrance of the lupins to follow the promise of the laurels. How charming was the curve of that brown, foam-flecked stream, as it rushed swiftly down, from pool to pool, under the ancient, overhanging elms and willows and sycamores! We gave ourselves to the current, and darted swiftly past the row of weather-beaten houses on the left bank, into the heart of the woods again.

Here the forest was dense, lofty, overarching. The tall silver maple, the black ash, the river birch, the swamp white oak, the sweet gum and the sour gum, and a score of other trees closed around the course of the stream as it swept along with full, swirling waters. The air was full of a diffused, tranquil green light, subdued yet joyous, through which flakes and beams of golden sunshine flickered and sifted downward, as if they were falling into some strange, ethereal medium—something half liquid and half aërial, midway between an atmosphere and the still depths of a fairy sea.

The spirit of enchantment was in the place; brooding in the delicate, luminous midday twilight; hushing the song of the strong-flowing river to a humming murmur; casting a spell of beautiful immobility on the slender flower-stalks and fern-fronds and trailing shrubberies of the undergrowth, while the young leaves of the tree-tops, far overhead, were quivering and dancing in the sunlight and the breeze. Here Oberon and Titania might sleep beneath a bower of motionless royal Osmunda. Here Puck might

152

have a noon-tide council with Peaseblossom, Cobweb, Moth, and Mustardseed, holding forth to them in whispers, beneath the green and purple sounding-board of a Jack-in-the-Pulpit. Here, even in this age of reason, the mystery of nature wove its magic round the curious mind of man,

> "*Annihilating all that's made,*
> *To a green thought in a green shade.*"

Do you remember how old Andrew Marvell goes on from those two lovely lines, in his poem?

> "*Here at the fountain's sliding foot,*
> *Or at some fruit-tree's mossy root,*
> *Casting the body's vest aside,*
> *My soul into the boughs does glide;*
> *There, like a bird, it sits and sings,*
> *Then whets and claps its silver wings,*
> *And, till prepared for longer flight,*
> *Waves in its plumes the various light.*"

There were many beautiful shrubs and bushes coming into bloom around us as we drifted down the stream. Two of the fairest bore the names of nymphs. One was called after Leucothoë, "the white goddess," and its curved racemes of tiny white bells hanging over the

153

water were worthy emblems of that pure queen who leaped into the sea with her babe in her arms to escape from the frenzy of Athamas. The other was named for Andromeda; and the great Linnæus, who gave the name, thus describes his thought in giving it: "*Andromeda polifolia* was now in its highest beauty, decorating the marshy grounds in a most agreeable manner. The flowers are quite blood-red before they expand, but when full-grown the corolla is of a flesh-colour. As I contemplated it, I could not help thinking of Andromeda as described by the poets; and the more I meditated upon their descriptions, the more applicable they seemed to the little plant before me. Andromeda is represented by them as a virgin of most exquisite and unrivalled charms. . . . "This plant is always fixed on some little turfy hillock in the midst of the swamps, as Andromeda herself was chained to the rock in the sea, which bathed her feet as the fresh water does the roots of the plant. Dragons and venomous serpents surrounded her, as toads and other reptiles frequent the abode of her vegetable resembler. As the distressed virgin cast down her face through excessive affliction, so does this rosy coloured flower hang its head. . . . At

154

length comes Perseus in the shape of summer,
dries up the surrounding water and destroys
the monsters."

But more lovely than any of the shrubs along
the river was that small tree known as the
sweet bay or the swamp laurel. Of course it is
not a laurel at all, but a magnolia (*Magnolia
glauca*), and its glistening leaves, dark green
above, silvery beneath, are set around the solitary flowers at the ends of the branches, like
backgrounds of malachite, to bring out the perfection of a blossom carved in fresh ivory.
What creamy petals are these, so thick, so tenderly curved around the cone-like heart of
the flower's fertility! They are slightly warm
within, so that your finger can feel the soft glow
in the centre of the blossoms. But it is not for
you to penetrate into the secret of their love
mystery. Leave that to the downy bee, the
soft-winged moth, the flying beetle, who, seeking their own pleasure, carry the life-bestowing
pollen from flower to flower. Your heavy hand
would bruise the soft flesh and discolor its
purity. Be content to feast your eyes upon its
beauty, and breathe its wonderful fragrance,
floating on the air like the breath of love in the
south and wild summer.

DAYS OFF

About the middle of the afternoon, after passing through miles of enchanted forest, unbroken by sign of human habitation, we

> *"Came unto a land*
> *In which it seemed always afternoon."*

Low-rolling ridges of gravel, clothed with pine and oak, came down along the river. The bank on the right rose higher, and, at a sharp angle in the stream, lifted itself into a bluff-like point. Opposite was the serpentine course of the Dead River, coiling through an open marsh-meadow. Below the junction of the two streams our own river flowed swiftly, through a straight reach, to the mouth of the still lagoon where Mare Run came in.

Here we made our second camp, on the point, among the pines and the hollies. For here, at last, we were in the heart of the land of laurels, which we had come to see. All along the river we had found some of them, just beginning to open their flowers, here and there. But above and below the mouth of the Dead River the banks and ridges, under the high shadow of the pines, were crowded with shining clumps of the *Kalmia latifolia*, and something in the soil and exposure, or perhaps even the single day of warm sunshine that had passed since we began

156

our voyage, had brought them already into the young flood of bloom.

I have seen the flame azaleas at their bright hour of consummation in the hill country of central Georgia—lakes of tranquil and splendid fire spreading far away through the rough-barked colonnades of the pineries. I have seen the thickets of great rhododendrons on the mountains of Pennsylvania in coronation week, when the magic of June covered their rich robes of darkest green with countless sceptres, crowns, and globes of white bloom divinely tinged with rose: superb, opulent, imperial flowers. I have seen the Magnolia Gardens near Charleston when their Arabian Nights' dream of colour was unfolding beneath the dark cypresses and moss-bannered live-oaks. I have seen the tulip and hyacinth beds of Holland rolled like a gorgeous carpet on the meadows beneath the feet of Spring; and the royal gardens of Kew in the month when the rose is queen of all the flowers. But never have I seen an efflorescence more lovely, more satisfying to the eye, than that of the high laurel along the shores of the unknown little river in South Jersey.

Cool, pure, and virginal in their beauty, the innumerable clusters of pink and white blossoms thronged the avenues of the pine woods, and ranged themselves along the hillsides and sloping banks, and trooped down by cape and promontory to reflect their young loveliness in the flowing stream. It was as if some quiet and shadowy region of solitude had been suddenly invaded by companies of maidens attired for a holiday and joyously confident of their simple charms. The dim woodland was illumined with the blush of conscious pleasure.

Seen at a distance the flower clusters look like big hemispheres of flushed snow. But examine them closely and you see that each of the rounded umbels is compounded of many separate blossoms—shallow, half-translucent cups poised on slender stems of pale green. The cup is white, tinted more or less deeply with rose-pink, the colour brightest along the rim and on the outside. The edge is scalloped into five points, and on the outer surface there are ten tiny projections around the middle of the cup. Looking within, you find that each of these is a little red hollow made to receive the crimson tip of a curving anther, cunningly bent like a spring, so that the least touch may loosen it and scatter the pollen. There is no flower in the world more exquisitely fashioned than this. It is the emblem of a rustic maid in the sweet prime of her morning.

158

THE LUPIN AND THE LAUREL

We were well content with our day's voyage and our parting camp on the river. We had done no harm; no accident had befallen us; we had seen many lovely things and heard music from warbler and vireo, thrush and wren, all day long. Even now a wood thrush closed his last descant in flutelike notes across the river. Night began silently to weave her dusky veil upon the vast loom of the forest. The pink glow had gone from the flower-masses around us; whitely they glimmered through the deepening shadows, and stood like gentle ghosts against the dark. To-morrow we must paddle down to the village where the railroad crosses the river, and hurry back to civilization and work. But to-night we were still very far off; and we should sleep at the foot of a pine-tree, beneath the stars, among the virgin laurels.

LITTLE RED TOM

LITTLE RED TOM

*₊*MY Uncle Peter was much interested in the war which broke out, when Roosevelt was President, among the professional nature-writers. He said that it was a civil war, and therefore a philosopher was bound to be regardful of it, because a civil war always involved subtle problems of psychology. He also said that it was a most uncivil war, and that the picturesque violence of the language employed on both sides was intrinsically noteworthy to a philologist, and therefore he felt obliged to follow it with care. When the Chief Magistrate of his native country took a hand in it, my Uncle Peter claimed that it had become a subject of national importance and that no true patriot could be indifferent to it. Finally he admitted, in a moment of confidence, that the real reason for his interest was the fact that so many of his friends were engaged in the strife, on both sides, and were being badly pummeled; and that he would like to take some part in it himself. I asked him what part. He answered that he proposed to himself the part of

peace-maker. I pointed out that this part is usually the most perilous and painful. He said that this should not deter him from doing his duty, and he added that he thought he could do it in such a way that no one could tell that he was doing it. A week later he brought me the following paper, which he called

THE TRAGEDY OF LITTLE RED TOM:

A Contribution to the Fight About Nature-Books.

He was the youngest of the family, a late-comer at the feast of life. Yet the rose-garlands on the table were not faded when he arrived, and the welcome that he received was not colder, indeed it was probably several degrees warmer, because he was so tardy, so young, so tiny.

There was room for him in the household circle; joyous affection and merry murmurs of contentment greeted his coming. His older brothers never breathed a word of jealousy or unkindness toward him. He grew peacefully under the shelter of mother-love; and it would have been difficult to foresee, in the rosy promise of his youth, the crimson tragedy in which his life ended.

How dull, how insensible to such things, most

164

men and women are! They go on their way, busily and happily, doing their work, seeking their daily food, enjoying their human pleasures, and never troubling themselves about the hidden and inarticulate sorrows of the universe. The hunter hunts, and the fisher fishes, with inconsiderate glee. A man kills a troublesome insect, he eats a juicy berry or a succulent oyster, without thinking of what his victims must feel.

But there are some tender and sensitive souls who are too fine for these callous joys. They no longer imagine that human emotions are confined to man. They reflect that every plant and every animal is doomed to die in some way which the average man would regard as distinctly unpleasant. To them the sight of a chicken-house is full of sorrowful suggestion, and a walk through a vegetable garden is like a funeral procession. They meditate upon the tragic side of all existence; and to them there will be nothing strange in this story of the tragedy of Little Red Tom.

You have guessed that he was called "red" on account of his colour. It was a family trait. All his brothers had it; and strange to say they were proud of it.

Most people are so foolish that they speak

with ridicule, or even with contempt of this colour, when it is personally evolved. Have you ever asked yourself why it is that the cold world alludes derisively to a "red-headed boy," or a "red-headed girl"? The language is different when the locks are of another hue. Then it is a "black-haired boy," or a "golden-haired girl." Is not the very word "red-headed," with its implied slur upon an innocent and gorgeous colour, an unconscious evidence of the unreasonable prejudice and hard insensibility of the human race?

Not so the family of Tom. The redder they grew the happier they were, and the more pride their mother took in them. But she herself was green. And so was little Tom, like all his brothers, when he made his first appearance in the world—green—very green.

Nestled against his mother's side, sheltered by her embracing arms, safe and happy in the quietude of her maternal care, he must have looked out upon the passing show with wonder and pleasure, while she instilled into him the lessons of wisdom and the warnings of destiny.

"Grow, my little one," we can imagine her saying to him, in her mysterious wordless language, "your first duty is to grow. Look at your brothers, how big and round and fat they are! I can hardly lift them. They did what I told them, and see what they have become. All by growing! Simple process! Even a babe can understand it. Grow, my Tommykin, grow! But don't try to grow red; first, you must grow big."

It is quite sure, and evident to every imaginative observer of nature, that Tommy's mother *must* have told him something like this, for this is precisely what he did—obedient, docile, clever little creature! How else could he have learned it, if she had not taught him? Who can trace the subtle avenues by which intelligence is communicated from the old to the young, the treasured lore of the ages handed down from one generation to another? But when we see the result, when the little one begins to do what its parents and grandparents have done, is it not evident that the teaching must have been given, though in some way beyond our ken? If Tommy's mother had not taught him, there is at least an even chance that he would have tried to grow red before he grew big. But he laid her lesson to heart, and day by day, week by week, his rotundity expanded, while his verdancy remained.

It was a very beautiful life that they lived in the garden; and if the thoughts and feelings that unfolded there could be known, perhaps they would seem even more wonderful than the things which the old German gardener cultivated. Away at one end were the beds of old-fashioned flowers: hollyhocks and phlox and stocks, coreopsis and calliopsis, calendula and campanula, fox-gloves and monks-hoods and lady-slippers. At the other end were the strawberry-bed and the asparagus-bed. In between, there were long rows of all kinds of vegetables and small fruits and fragrant herbs.

Who can tell what ideas and emotions were stirring in those placid companies of leguminous comrades? What aspirations toward a loftier life in the climbing beans? What high spirits in the corn? What light and airy dreams on the asparagus-bed? What philosophy among the sage? Imagine what great schemes were hatching among the egg-plants, and what hot feelings stung the peppers when the raspberries crowded them!

Tommy, from his central place in the garden, must have felt the agitation of this mimic world around him. Many a time, no doubt, he was tempted to give himself up to one or another of the contiguous influences, and throw himself into the social tide for "one glorious hour of crowded life." But his mother always held him back.

LITTLE RED TOM

"No, my Tommykin, stay with me. It is not for you to climb a pole like a bean or wave in the wind like an asparagus stalk, or rasp your neighbours like a raspberry. Be modest, be natural, be true to yourself. Stay with me and grow fat."

When the sunshine of the long July days flooded the garden, glistening on the silken leaves of the corn, wilting the potato-blossoms, unfolding the bright yellow flowers of the okra and the melon, Tom would fain have pushed himself out into the full tide of light and heat. But his mother bent tenderly over him.

"Not yet, my child; it is not time for you to bear the heat of the day. A little shade is good for you. Let me cover you. It is too soon for you to be sunburned."

When the plumping afternoon showers came down, refreshing leaf and root of every plant, Tom shrank from the precipitate inundation.

"Mother, I'm all wet. I want to come in out of the rain."

But the mother knew what was good for him. So she held him out bravely while the streaming drops washed him; and she taught him how to draw in the moisture which she gathered for his nourishment.

In late August a change began to come over

his complexion. His verdant brilliancy was "sicklied o'er with a pale cast of thought," whitish, yellowish, nondescript. A foolish human mother would have been alarmed and would have hurried to the medicine closet for a remedy for biliousness. Not so Tom's wise parent. She knew that the time had come for him to grow red. She let him have his own way now about being out in the sunshine. She even thrust him gently forth into the full light, withdrawing the shelter that she had cast around him. Slowly, gradually, but surely the bright crimson hue spread over him, until the illumination was complete, and the mother felt that he was the most beautiful of her children —not the largest, but round and plump and firm and glowing red as a ruby.

Then the mother-heart knew that the perils of life were near at hand for Little Red Tom. Many of his brothers had already been torn from her by the cruel hand of fate and had disappeared into the unknown.

"Where have they gone to?" wondered Tom. But his mother could not tell him. All that she could do was to warn him of the unseen dangers that surrounded him, and prepare him to meet them.

"Listen, my child, and do as I tell you. When

you hear a step on the garden path, that means
danger; and when a thing with wings flies
around me and comes near to you, that means
danger too. But I will teach you how to avoid
it. I will give you three signs.

"The first sign is a rustling noise that I will
make when a bird comes near to you. That
means *droop*. Let yourself down behind the
wire netting that I lean on, and then the bird
will be afraid to come close enough to peck at
you. The second sign is a trembling that you
will feel in my arms when the gardener comes
along the walk. That means *snuggle*. Hide
yourself as close to me as you can. The third
sign—well, I will tell you the third sign to-
morrow evening, for now I am tired."

In the early morning of a bright September
day, while the dew was still heavy on the leaves
and the grass, and the gossamer cobwebs glistened with little diamonds, a hungry robin flew
into the garden, and Tom heard the signal
"Droop!" So he let himself down behind the
woven wire, and the robin put his head on one
side and looked at Tom greedily, and flew on to
find a breakfast elsewhere.

A little before noon, when the sun was shining broadly and the silken tassels of the corn
were shrivelling up into make-believe tobacco

for bad little boys to smoke, there was a heavy
step on the garden walk, and Tom felt the signal *"Snuggle!"* Then he hugged as close as
he could to his mother's side, and the gardener
with his sharp knife cut off all Tom's surviving
brothers and put them into a box full of vegetables. But he did not see Tom, hidden close
and safe.

How glad the mother must have been, and
how much Tom must have loved her as he
remembered all her wise lessons! It was a long
beautiful afternoon that they spent together,
filled with pleasant reminiscences, touched by
no shadow of gloom, no dream of parting. A
golden afternoon—the last!

Just before sunset, a fair creature, clothed in
white, came into the garden. She moved for a
while among the flowers, her yellow hair gleaming in the low rays of the sun, her eyes bluer
than forget-me-nots. Who could think that
such a creature would be cruel or heartless?
Who could dream that she would pursue her
pleasure at the cost of pain to the innocent?
Who could imagine that she would take life to
feed her own?

Gently and daintily she came down the garden walk, past the raspberry patch, past the
tall rows of corn, past the egg-plants and the

peppers, with steps so light that the ground hardly felt them, with bright eyes glancing from side to side—yes, with all these, and also with a remorseless purpose in her heart and a basket half full of cut flowers on her arm.

No signal to *droop* or *snuggle* came to Tom. The third signal—ah, that he had not yet learned! So he basked in the sunlight as the lovely apparition drew near to him. She looked at him with delight. She put out her delicate hand to embrace him. Then, without a tremor, she tore him ruthlessly from his mother's grasp, from the home that he loved, and dropped him into her basket.

"Oh, you little red beauty!" she cried. "You are just what I wanted to fill up my tomato salad."

That night, as she sat at supper, with her father and mother and brother and sisters, she was smiling and serene, for the table was well furnished, and the feast was merry. There was white bread that had been ground from thousands of innocent blades of wheat, once waving in the sunlight, and a juicy fish that had been lured and unwillingly drawn from the crystal waters. There was a brace of grouse that had been snatched away from their feeding-grounds among the spicy berries in the woods. And there was poor Little Red Tom, in the centre of the salad, surrounded by crisp lettuce leaves and dressed to the queen's taste.

Are there not some who would have shed tears at that sight, and lamented even while they ate? But do you suppose the young girl was one of that kind? Do you imagine that she thought she had played a part in a tragedy? Not a bit of it. She was simply grateful that her salad was so good, and glad that the others liked it.

Moral

Reader, if you would not be like this young girl, you must read and believe——*

* Note: I regret to state that my Uncle Peter's manuscript broke off at this point.

SILVERHORNS

SILVERHORNS

THE railway station of Bathurst, New Brunswick, did not look particularly merry at two o'clock of a late September morning. There was an easterly haar driving in from the *Baie des Chaleurs* and the darkness was so saturated with chilly moisture that an honest downpour of rain would have been a relief. Two or three depressed and somnolent travellers yawned in the waiting-room, which smelled horribly of smoky lamps. The telegraph instrument in the ticket-office clicked spasmodically for a minute, and then relapsed into a gloomy silence. The imperturbable station-master was tipped back against the wall in a wooden armchair, with his feet on the table, and his mind sunk in an old Christmas number of *The Cowboy Magazine*. The express-agent, in the baggage-room, was going over his last week's way-bills and accounts by the light of a lantern, trying to locate an error, and sighing profanely to himself as he failed to find it. A wooden trunk tied with rope, a couple of dingy canvas bags, a long box marked "Fresh Fish! Rush!" and two large

177

leather portmanteaus with brass fittings were piled on the luggage-truck at the far end of the platform; and beside the door of the waiting-room, sheltered by the overhanging eaves, was a neat travelling bag, with a gun-case and a rod-case leaning against the wall. The wet rails glittered dimly northward and southward away into the night. A few blurred lights glimmered from the village across the bridge.

Dudley Hemenway had observed all these features of the landscape with silent dissatisfaction, as he smoked steadily up and down the platform, waiting for the Maritime Express. It is usually irritating to arrive at the station on time for a train on the Intercolonial Railway. The arrangement is seldom mutual; and sometimes yesterday's train does not come along until to-morrow afternoon. Moreover, Hemenway was inwardly discontented with the fact that he was coming out of the woods instead of going in. "Coming out" always made him a little unhappy, whether his expedition had been successful or not. He did not like the thought that it was all over; and he had the very bad habit, at such times, of looking ahead and computing the slowly lessening number of chances that were left to him.

"Sixty odd years—I may live to be that old

and keep my shooting sight," he said to himself.
"That would give me a couple of dozen more
camping trips. It's a short allowance. I wonder if any of them will be more lucky than this
one. This makes the seventh year I've tried to
get a moose; and the odd trick has gone against
me every time."

He tossed away the end of his cigar, which
made a little trail of sparks as it rolled along
the sopping platform, and turned to look in
through the window of the ticket-office. Something in the agent's attitude of literary absorp-
tion aggravated him. He went round to the
door and opened it.

"Don't you know or care when this train is
coming?"

"Nope," said the man placidly.

"Well, when? What's the matter with her?
When is she due?"

"Doo twenty minits ago," said the man.
"Forty minits late down to Noocastle. Git
here quatter to three, ef nothin' more happens."

"But what has happened already? What's
wrong with the beastly old road, anyhow?"

"Freight-car skipped the track," said the
man, "up to Charlo. Everythin' hung up an'
kinder goin' slow till they git the line clear.
Dunno nothin' more."

DAYS OFF

With this conclusive statement the agent seemed to disclaim all responsibility for the future of impatient travellers, and dropped his mind back into the magazine again. Hemenway lit another cigar and went into the baggage-room to smoke with the expressman. It was nearly three o'clock when they heard the far-off shriek of the whistle sounding up from the south; then, after an interval, the puffing of the engine on the up-grade; then the faint ringing of the rails, the increasing clatter of the train, and the blazing headlight of the locomotive swept slowly through the darkness, past the platform. The engineer was leaning on one arm, with his head out of the cab-window, and as he passed he nodded and waved his hand to Hemenway. The conductor also nodded and hurried into the ticket-office, where the tick-tack of a conversation by telegraph was soon under way. The black porter of the Pullman car was looking out from the vestibule, and when he saw Hemenway his sleepy face broadened into a grin reminiscent of many generous tips.

"Howdy, Mr. Hennigray," he cried; "glad to see yo' ag'in, sah! I got yo' section alright, sah! Lemme take yo' things, sah! Train gwine to stop hy'eh fo' some time yet, I reckon."

"Well, Charles," said Hemenway, "you take

180

my things and put them in the car. Careful
with that gun now! The Lord only knows how
much time this train's going to lose. I'm going
ahead to see the engineer."

Angus McLeod was a grizzle-bearded Scotchman who had run a locomotive on the Intercolonial ever since the road was cut through the
woods from New Brunswick to Quebec. Everyone who travelled often on that line knew him,
and all who knew him well enough to get below
his rough crust, liked him for his big heart.

"Hallo, McLeod," said Hemenway as he came
up through the darkness, "is that you?"

"It's nane else," answered the engineer as he
stepped down from his cab and shook hands
warmly. "Hoo are ye, Dud, an' whaur hae ye
been murderin' the innocent beasties noo?
Hae ye killt yer moose yet? Ye've been chasin'
him these mony years."

"Not much murdering," replied Hemenway.
"I had a queer trip this time—away up the
Nepissiguit, with old McDonald. You know
him, don't you?"

"Fine do I ken Rob McDonald, an' a guid
mon he is. Hoo was it that ye couldna slaugh-
ter stacks o' moose wi' him to help ye? Did ye
see nane at all?"

"Plenty, and one with the biggest horns in

181

the world! But that's a long story, and there's no time to tell it now."

"Time to burrrn, Dud, nae fear o' it! 'Twill be an hour afore the line's clear to Charlo an' they lat us oot o' this. Come awa' up into the cab, mon, an' tell us yer tale. 'Tis couthy an' warm in the cab, an' I'm willin' to leesten to yer bluidy advaintures."

So the two men clambered up into the engineer's seat. Hemenway gave McLeod his longest and strongest cigar, and filled his own briarwood pipe. The rain was now pattering gently on the roof of the cab. The engine hissed and sizzled patiently in the darkness. The fragrant smoke curled steadily from the glowing tip of the cigar; but the pipe went out half a dozen times while Hemenway was telling the story of Silverhorns.

"We went up the river to the big rock, just below Indian Falls. There we made our main camp, intending to hunt on Forty-two Mile Brook. There's quite a snarl of ponds and bogs at the head of it, and some burned hills over to the west, and it's very good moose country.

"But some other party had been there before us, and we saw nothing on the ponds, except two cow moose and a calf. Coming out the next morning we got a fine deer on the old wood road—a beautiful head. But I have plenty of deer-heads already."

"Bonny creature!" said McLeod. "An' what did ye do wi' it, when ye had murdered it?"

"Ate it, of course. I gave the head to Billy Boucher, the cook. He said he could get ten dollars for it. The next evening we went to one of the ponds again, and Injun Pete tried to 'call' a moose for me. But it was no good. McDonald was disgusted with Pete's calling; said it sounded like the bray of a wild ass of the wilderness. So the next day we gave up calling and travelled the woods over toward the burned hills.

"In the afternoon McDonald found an enormous moose-track; he thought it looked like a bull's track, though he wasn't quite positive. But then, you know, a Scotchman never likes to commit himself, except about theology or politics."

"Humph!" grunted McLeod in the darkness, showing that the stroke had counted.

"Well, we went on, following that track through the woods, for an hour or two. It was a terrible country, I tell you: tamarack swamps, and spruce thickets, and windfalls, and all kinds of misery. Presently we came out on a bare rock on the burned hillside, and there, across a ravine, we could see the animal lying down, just below the trunk of a big dead spruce that had fallen. The beast's head and neck were hidden by some bushes, but the foreshoulder and side were in clear view, about two hundred and fifty yards away. McDonald seemed to be inclined to think that it was a bull and that I ought to shoot. So I shot, and knocked splinters out of the spruce log. We could see them fly. The animal got up quickly, and looked at us for a moment, shaking her long ears; then the huge, unmitigated cow vamoosed into the brush. McDonald remarked that it was 'a varra fortunate shot, almaist providaintial!' And so it was; for if it had gone six inches lower, and the news had gotten out at Bathurst, it would have cost me a fine of two hundred dollars."

"Ye did weel, Dud," puffed McLeod; "varra weel indeed—for the coo!"

"After that," continued Hemenway, "of course my nerve was a little shaken, and we went back to the main camp on the river, to rest over Sunday. That was all right, wasn't it, Mac?"

"Aye!" replied McLeod, who was a strict member of the Presbyterian church at Moncton. "That was surely a varra safe thing to do.

Even a hunter, I'm thinkin', wouldna like to be breakin' twa commandments in ane day—the foorth and the saxth!"

"Perhaps not. It's enough to break one, as you do once a fortnight when you run your train into Rivière du Loup Sunday morning. How's that, you old Calvinist?"

"Dudley, ma son," said the engineer, "dinna argue a point that ye canna understond. There's guid an' suffeecient reasons for the train. But ye'll ne'er be claimin' that moose-huntin' is a wark o' neecessity or maircy?"

"No, no, of course not; but then, you see, barring Sundays, we felt that it was necessary to do all we could to get a moose, just for the sake of our reputations. Billy, the cook, was particularly strong about it. He said that an old woman in Bathurst, a kind of fortune-teller, had told him that he was going to have '*la bonne chance*' on this trip. He wanted to try his own mouth at 'calling.' He had never really done it before. But he had been practising all winter in imitation of a tame cow moose that Johnny Moreau had, and he thought he could make the sound '*b'en bon*.' So he got the birch-bark horn and gave us a sample of his skill. McDonald told me privately that it was 'nae sa bad; a deal better than Pete's feckless bellow.' We

185

agreed to leave the Indian to keep the camp (after locking up the whiskey-flask in my bag), and take Billy with us on Monday to 'call' at Hogan's Pond.

"It's a small bit of water, about three-quarters of a mile long and four hundred yards across, and four miles back from the river. There is no trail to it, but a blazed line runs part of the way, and for the rest you follow up the little brook that runs out of the pond. We stuck up our shelter in a hollow on the brook, half a mile below the pond, so that the smoke of our fire would not drift over the hunting-ground, and waited till five o'clock in the afternoon. Then we went up to the pond, and took our position in a clump of birch-trees on the edge of the open meadow that runs round the east shore. Just at dark Billy began to call, and it was beautiful. You know how it goes. Three short grunts, and then a long ooooo-aaaa-ooooh, winding up with another grunt! It sounded lonelier than a love-sick hippopotamus on the house-top. It rolled and echoed over the hills as if it would wake the dead.

"There was a fine moon shining, nearly full, and a few clouds floating by. Billy called, and called, and called again. The air grew colder and colder; light frost on the meadow-grass; our teeth were chattering, fingers numb.

"Then we heard a bull give a short bawl, away off to the southward. Presently we could hear his horns knock against the trees, far up on the hill. McDonald whispered, 'He's comin',' and Billy gave another call.

"But it was another bull that answered, back of the north end of the pond, and pretty soon we could hear him rapping along through the woods. Then everything was still. 'Call agen,' says McDonald, and Billy called again.

"This time the bawl came from another bull, on top of the western hill, straight across the pond. It seemed to start up the other two bulls, and we could hear all three of them thrashing along, as fast as they could come, towards the pond. 'Call agen, a wee one,' says McDonald, trembling with joy. And Billy called a little, seducing call, with two grunts at the end.

"Well, sir, at that, a cow and a calf came rushing down through the brush not two hundred yards away from us, and the three bulls went splash into the water, one at the south end, one at the north end, and one on the west shore. 'Lord,' whispers McDonald, 'it's a mee-nadgerie!'"

"Dud," said the engineer, getting down to open the furnace door a crack, "this is mair than murder ye're comin' at; it's a buitchery—or else it's juist a pack o' lees."

187

"I give you my word," said Hemenway, "it's all true as the catechism. But let me go on. The cow and the calf only stayed in the water a few minutes, and then ran back through the woods. But the three bulls went sloshing around in the pond as if they were looking for something. We could hear them, but we could not see any of them, for the sky had clouded up, and they kept far away from us. Billy tried another short call, but they did not come any nearer. McDonald whispered that he thought the one in the south end might be the biggest, and he might be feeding, and the two others might be young bulls, and they might be keeping away because they were afraid of the big one. This seemed reasonable; and I said that I was going to crawl around the meadow to the south end. 'Keep near a tree,' says Mac; and I started.

"There was a deep trail, worn by animals, through the high grass; and in this I crept along on my hands and knees. It was very wet and muddy. My boots were full of cold water. After ten minutes I came to a little point running out into the pond, and one young birch growing on it. Under this I crawled, and rising up on my knees looked over the top of the grass and bushes.

SILVERHORNS

"There, in a shallow bay, standing knee-deep in the water, and rooting up the lily-stems with his long, pendulous nose, was the biggest and blackest bull moose in the world. As he pulled the roots from the mud and tossed up his dripping head I could see his horns—four and a half feet across, if they were an inch, and the palms shining like silver tea-trays in the moonlight. I tell you, old Silverhorns was the most beautiful monster I ever saw.

"But he was too far away to shoot by that dim light, so I left my birch-tree and crawled along toward the edge of the bay. A breath of wind must have blown across me to him, for he lifted his head, sniffed, grunted, came out of the water, and began to trot slowly along the trail which led past me. I knelt on one knee and tried to take aim. A black cloud came over the moon. I couldn't see either of the sights on the gun. But when the bull came opposite to me, about fifty yards off, I blazed away at a venture.

"He reared straight up on his hind legs—it looked as if he rose fifty feet in the air—wheeled, and went walloping along the trail, around the south end of the pond. In a minute he was lost in the woods. Good-by, Silverhorns!"

"Ye tell it weel," said McLeod, reaching out

for a fresh cigar, "fegs! Ah doot Sir Walter himsel' couldna impruve upon it. An' sae thot's the way ye didna murder puir Seelverhorrns? It's a tale I'm joyfu' to be hearin'."

"Wait a bit," Hemenway answered. "That's not the end, by a long shot. There's worse to follow. The next morning we returned to the pond at daybreak, for McDonald thought I might have wounded the moose. We searched the bushes and the woods where he went out very carefully, looking for drops of blood on his trail."

"Bluid!" groaned the engineer. "Hech, mon, wouldna that come nigh to mak' ye greet, to find the beast's red bluid splashed ower the leaves, and think o' him staggerin' on thro' the forest, drippin' the heart oot o' him wi' every step?"

"But we didn't find any blood, you old sentimentalist. That shot in the dark was a clear miss. We followed the trail by broken bushes and footprints, for half a mile, and then came back to the pond and turned to go down through the edge of the woods to the camp.

"It was just after sunrise. I was walking a few yards ahead, McDonald next, and Billy last. Suddenly he looked around to the left, gave a low whistle and dropped to the ground, pointing northward. Away at the head of the pond, beyond the glitter of the sun on the water, the big blackness of Silverhorns' head and body was pushing through the bushes, dripping with dew.

"Each of us flopped down behind the nearest shrub as if we had been playing squat-tag. Billy had the birch-bark horn with him, and he gave a low, short call. Silverhorns heard it, turned, and came parading slowly down the western shore, now on the sand-beach, now splashing through the shallow water. We could see every motion and hear every sound. He marched along as if he owned the earth, swinging his huge head from side to side and grunting at each step.

"You see, we were just in the edge of the woods, strung along the south end of the pond, Billy nearest the west shore, where the moose was walking, McDonald next, and I last, perhaps fifteen yards farther to the east. It was a fool arrangement, but we had no time to think about it. McDonald whispered that I should wait until the moose came close to us and stopped.

"So I waited. I could see him swagger along the sand and step out around the fallen logs. The nearer he came the bigger his horns looked; each palm was like a giant's silver fish-fork

with twenty prongs. Then he went out of my
sight for a minute as he passed around a little
bay in the southwest corner, getting nearer and
nearer to Billy. But I could still hear his steps
distinctly—slosh, slosh, slosh—thud, thud, thud
(the grunting had stopped)—closer came the
sound, until it was directly behind the dense
green branches of a fallen balsam-tree, not
twenty feet away from Billy. Then suddenly
the noise ceased. I could hear my own heart
pounding at my ribs, but nothing else. And of
Silverhorns not hair nor hide was visible. It
looked as if he must be a Boojum, and had the
power to

'*Softly and silently vanish away.*'

"Billy and Mac were beckoning to me fiercely
and pointing to the green balsam-top. I gripped
my rifle and started to creep toward them. A
little twig, about as thick as the tip of a fishing-
rod, cracked under my knee. There was a terrible crash behind the balsam, a plunging
through the underbrush and a rattling among
the branches, a lumbering gallop up the hill
through the forest, and Silverhorns was gone
into the invisible.

"He had stopped behind the tree because he
smelled the grease on Billy's boots. As he

stood there, hesitating, Billy and Mac could see his shoulder and his side through a gap in the branches—a dead-easy shot. But so far as I was concerned, he might as well have been in Alaska. I told you that the way we had placed ourselves was a fool arrangement. But McDonald would not say anything about it, except to express his conviction that *it was not predestinated we should get that moose*."

"Ah didna ken auld Rob had sae much theology aboot him," commented McLeod. "But noo I'm thinkin' ye went back to yer main camp, an' lat puir Seelverhoorns live oot his life?"

"Not much, did we! For now we knew that he wasn't badly frightened by the adventure of the night before, and that we might get another chance at him. In the afternoon it began to rain; and it poured for forty-eight hours. We cowered in our shelter before a smoky fire, and lived on short rations of crackers and dried prunes—it was a hungry time."

"But wasna there slathers o' food at the main camp? Ony fule wad ken eneugh to gae doon to the river an' tak' a guid fill-up."

"But that wasn't what we wanted. It was Silverhorns. Billy and I made McDonald stay, and Thursday afternoon, when the clouds broke away, we went back to the pond to have a last try at turning our luck.

"This time we took our positions with great care, among some small spruces on a point that ran out from the southern meadow. I was farthest to the west; McDonald (who had also brought his gun) was next; Billy, with the horn, was farthest away from the point where he thought the moose would come out. So Billy began to call, very beautifully. The long echoes went bellowing over the hills. The afternoon was still and the setting sun shone through a light mist, like a ball of red gold.

"Fifteen minutes after sundown Silverhorns gave a loud bawl from the western ridge and came crashing down the hill. He cleared the bushes two or three hundred yards to our left with a leap, rushed into the pond, and came wading around the south shore toward us. The bank here was rather high, perhaps four feet above the water, and the mud below it was deep, so that the moose sank in to his knees. I give you my word, as he came along there was nothing visible to Mac and me except his ears and his horns. Everything else was hidden below the bank.

"There were we behind our little spruce-trees. And there was Silverhorns, standing still now, right in front of us. And all that Mac and I could see were those big ears and those magnificent antlers, appearing and disappearing as he lifted and lowered his head. It was a fearful situation. And there was Billy, with his birch-bark hooter, forty yards below us—he could see the moose perfectly.

"I looked at Mac, and he looked at me. He whispered something about predestination. Then Billy lifted his horn and made ready to give a little soft grunt, to see if the moose wouldn't move along a bit, just to oblige us. But as Billy drew in his breath, one of those tiny fool flies that are always blundering around a man's face flew straight down his throat. Instead of a call he burst out in a furious, strangling fit of coughing. The moose gave a snort, and a wild leap in the water, and galloped away under the bank, the way he had come. Mac and I both fired at his vanishing ears and horns, but of course——"

"All aboooard!" The conductor's shout rang along the platform.

"Line's clear," exclaimed McLeod, rising. "Noo we'll be off! Wull ye stay here wi' me, or gang awa' back to yer bed?"

"Here," answered Hemenway, not budging from his place on the bench.

195

The bell clanged, and the powerful machine puffed out on its flaring way through the night. Faster and faster came the big explosive breaths, until they blended in a long steady roar, and the train was sweeping northward at forty miles an hour. The clouds had broken; the night had grown colder; the gibbous moon gleamed over the vast and solitary landscape. It was a different thing to Hemenway, riding in the cab of the locomotive, from an ordinary journey in the passenger-car or an unconscious ride in the sleeper. Here he was on the crest of motion, at the fore-front of speed, and the quivering engine with the long train behind it seemed like a living creature leaping along the track. It responded to the labour of the fireman and the touch of the engineer almost as if it could think and feel. Its pace quickened without a jar; its great eye pierced the silvery space of moonlight with a shaft of blazing yellow; the rails sang before it and trembled behind it; it was an obedient and joyful monster, conquering distance and devouring darkness.

On the wide level barrens beyond the Tete-a-Gouche River the locomotive reached its best speed, purring like a huge cat and running smoothly. McLeod leaned back on his bench with a satisfied air.

"She's doin' fine, the nicht," said he. "Ah'm thinkin', whiles, o' yer auld Seelverhorrns. Whaur is he noo? Awa' up on Hogan's Pond, gallantin' around i' the licht o' the mune wi' a lady moose, an' the gladness juist bubblin' in his hairt. Ye're no sorry that he's leevin' yet, are ye, Dud?"

"Well," answered Hemenway slowly, between the puffs of his pipe, "I can't say I'm sorry that he's alive and happy, though I'm not glad that I lost him. But he did his best, the old rogue; he played a good game, and he deserved to win. Where he is now nobody can tell. He was travelling like a streak of lightning when I last saw him. By this time he may be——"

"What's yon?" cried McLeod, springing up. Far ahead, in the narrow apex of the converging rails, stood a black form, motionless, mysterious. McLeod grasped the whistle-cord. The black form loomed higher in the moonlight and was clearly silhouetted against the horizon—a big moose standing across the track. They could see his grotesque head, his shadowy horns, his high, sloping shoulders. The engineer pulled the cord. The whistle shrieked loud and long.

The moose turned and faced the sound. The glare of the headlight fascinated, challenged, angered him. There he stood defiant, front

197

feet planted wide apart, head lowered, gazing
steadily at the unknown enemy that was rushing toward him. He was the monarch of the
wilderness. There was nothing in the world
that he feared, except those strange-smelling
little beasts on two legs who crept around
through the woods and shot fire out of sticks.
This was surely not one of those treacherous
animals, but some strange new creature that
dared to shriek at him and try to drive him out
of its way. He would not move. He would
try his strength against this big yellow-eyed
beast.

"Losh!" cried McLeod; "he's gaun' to fecht
us!" and he dropped the cord, grabbed the
levers, and threw the steam off and the brakes
on hard. The heavy train slid groaning and
jarring along the track. The moose never
stirred. The fire smouldered in his small narrow eyes. His black crest was bristling. As
the engine bore down upon him, not a rod away,
he reared high in the air, his antlers flashing in
the blaze, and struck full at the headlight with
his immense fore feet. There was a shattering
of glass, a crash, a heavy shock, and the train
slid on through the darkness, lit only by the
moon.

Thirty or forty yards beyond, the momentum

was exhausted and the engine came to a stop. Hemenway and McLeod clambered down and ran back, with the other trainmen and a few of the passengers. The moose was lying in the ditch beside the track, stone dead and frightfully shattered. But the great head and the vast, spreading antlers were intact.

"Seelver-horrns, sure eneugh!" said McLeod, bending over him. "He was crossin' frae the Nepissiguit to the Jacquet; but he didna get across. Weel, Dud, are ye glad? Ye hae killt yer first moose!"

"Yes," said Hemenway, "it's my first moose. But it's your first moose, too. And I think it's our last. Ye gods, what a fighter!"

NOTIONS ABOUT NOVELS

NOTIONS ABOUT NOVELS

"YOU must write a novel," said my Uncle Peter to the young Man of Letters. "The novel is the literary form in which the psychological conditions of interest are most easily discovered and met. It appeals directly to the reader's self-consciousness, and invites him to fancy how fine a figure he would cut in more picturesque circumstances than his own. When it simplifies great events, as Stevenson said it must, it produces the feeling of power; and when it dignifies the commonplace, as Schopenhauer said it ought to, it produces the sense of importance. People like to imagine themselves playing on a large stage. The most humdrum of men would be pleased to act a hero's part, if it could be done without risk or effort; and the plainest of women has the capacity to enjoy, at least in fancy, a greater variety in the affair of love than real life is likely to furnish. Novels give these unsatisfied souls their opportunity. That is why fiction is so popular. You must take advantage of the laws of the human mind if you want to be a successful author. Write a novel."

DAYS OFF

This protracted remark was patiently received by the little company of friends, who were sitting on a rocky eminence of the York Harbor Golf Links (near the seventh hole, which was called, for obvious reasons, "Götterdämmerung"). My Uncle Peter's right to make long speeches was conceded. In him they did not seem criminal, because they were evidently necessary. Moreover, in this case, the majority agreed with him, and therefore were not tempted to interrupt.

"A novel," said the Publisher, "will bear ten times as much advertising as any other kind of book. This is a fact."

"A novel," said the Critic, "is the most highly developed type of literature. Therefore, it is the fittest to survive. This is a theory. And I should like——"

But the Critic did not share the Philosopher's long-speech prerogative. His audience was inclined to limit him to the time when he could be pungent.

The Business Man broke in upon him: "A novel is good because it is just plain reading—no theories or explanations—or at least, if there are any, you can skip them."

"Novels," said the Doctor of Divinity solemnly, "are valuable because they give an in-

204

sight into life. I deprecate the vice of excessive novel-reading in young persons. But for myself I wish that there were more really interesting novels to read. Most of the old ones I have read already."

A smile flickered around the circle. "What do you call old?" asked the Cynic. "Have you read *The Vulgarities of Antoinette?*"

"Nonsense," said the Publisher; "some novels grow as old in a twelvemonth as others do in a decade. A book is not really aged until it ceases to be advertised. *The Celestial Triplets*, for example. But fortunately it is a poor year that does not produce at least three new novelists of distinction."

"For my part," said the True Story Teller, seated on her throne among the rocks and dispensing gentle influence like the silent sweetness of the summer afternoon, "for my part, I am not sure that fiction is the only kind of literature worth reading. Essays, biography, history and poetry still have their attractions for me. But what I should like to know is what made one kind of novel so popular yesterday, and what puts another kind in its place to-day, and what kind is likely to last forever? What gives certain novels their amazing vogue?"

"A new public," answered the Cynic. "Popular education has done it. Fifty years ago thinking and reading went together. But nowadays reading is the most familiar amusement of the thoughtless. It is the new public that buys four hundred thousand copies of a novel in a single year."

"A striking explanation," said the Critic, "but you know De Quincey said practically the same thing more than fifty years ago in his essay on Oliver Goldsmith. Yet the sale of *The Prude of Pimlico* exceeds the sale of the leading novel of De Quincey's day by at least five hundred per cent. How do you explain that?"

"Very simply," said the Cynic. "A thousand *per centum* increase in the new public; stock of intelligence still more freely watered."

"But you are not answering my question about the different kinds of novels," said the lady. "Tell me why the types of fiction change."

"Fashion, dear lady," replied the Cynic. "It is like tight sleeves and loose sleeves. People feel comfortable when they wear what everybody is wearing and read what everybody is reading. The art of modern advertising is an appeal to the instinct of imitation. Our friend the Publisher has become a millionaire by discovering that the same law governs the sale of books and of dry-goods."

NOTIONS ABOUT NOVELS

"Not at all," interrupted the Critic; "your explanation is too crude for satire and too shallow for science. There is a regular evolution in fiction. First comes the external type, the novel of plot; then the internal type, the novel of character; then the social type, the novel of problem and purpose. The development proceeds from outward to inward, from objective to subjective, from simplicity to complexity."

"But," said the lady, "if I remember rightly, the facts happened the other way. *Pamela* and *Joseph Andrews* and *Caleb Williams* are character novels; *Waverley* and *Ivanhoe* are adventure novels. Kingsley wrote *Yeast* and *Alton Locke* before *Westward Ho!* and *Hypatia*. *Bleak House* and *Uncle Tom's Cabin* are older than *Lorna Doone* and *David Balfour*. The day before yesterday it was all character-sketching, mainly Scotch; the day before that it was all problem-solving, chiefly religious; yesterday it was all adventure-seeking, called historical because it seems highly improbable; and to-day it is a mixture of automobile-journeys and slum-life. It looks to me as if there must be somebody always ready to read some kind of fiction, but his affections are weather-cocky."

"I don't object to a few characters in a novel,"

said the Man of Business, "provided they do something interesting."

"Right," said the Publisher; "the public always knows what is interesting, provided it is properly pointed out. Now here is a little list of our most profitable new books: a story of a beautiful Cow-boy, a Kentucky love-tale, a narrative of the Second Crusade, a romance about an imaginary princess and two motor-cars, a modern society story with vivid descriptions of the principal New York restaurants and Monte Carlo—all of these have passed the forty-thousand line. We send out the list with a statement to that effect, and advise people not to lose the chance of reading books that have aroused so much interest."

"It seems to me," put in the Doctor of Divinity, "that some of the modern books do not give me as much insight into life as I should like. I perused *The Prisoner on a Bender* the other day without getting a single illustration for a sermon. But I continue to read novels from a sense of duty, to keep in touch with my young people."

"I think," began my Uncle Peter (and this solemn announcement made everyone attentive), "I think you have failed to discern a certain law of periodicity which governs the formal variations of fiction. This periodicity is natural to the human mind, and it also has relations to profound social movements. The popularity of the novels of Fielding, Richardson, and Smollett, whose characters were mainly drawn from humble life, was due to the rise of the same spirit of democracy that produced the American and French Revolutions. The reaction to the romantic and historical novel, under Scott and his followers, was a revival of the aristocratic spirit. It took a historical form because the past had been made vivid to the popular imagination by the great historians of the eighteenth century. The purpose novels, which took the lead in the middle of the nineteenth century, were another reaction, and came out of the social ferment of the times. The general pictures of society and manners which followed were written for a public that was fairly well-to-do and contented with itself. The later realistic studies of life in its lowest forms were the offspring of the scientific spirit. And the latest reaction to the novel of adventure, with its emphasis on daring and virility, is connected with the remarkable revival of imperialism. But while fiction is specifically the most transient of forms, generically it is the most permanent. Therefore, our young Man of Letters must write a novel. That is what the public wants."

"Yes," cried the Publisher, "a novel of adventure in Cromwell's time. That period is up, just now, and has not been worked out."

"A novel of purpose," said the Critic; "that is the highest type of fiction."

"A novel of character," said the Cynic. "A change in fashion is due. Take the President of a Trust for your hero, and make him repent under the pressure of the Social Boycott. The public loves surprises."

"Why not write the Great American Novel?" said the Doctor of Divinity. "I have heard several demands for it."

"A good love story," said the Man of Business, "or perhaps a detective story, would be the best thing to sell."

"The one point on which your friends seem agreed," said the True Story Teller, with a smile, "is that the public gives you an order for a novel."

"Well, you know, I have written one already," answered the young Man of Letters, very quietly.

"Why didn't you tell us?" chorused the others. "Why haven't you published it?"

He hesitated a moment before answering: "It did not seem to me good enough."

"My young friend," said the Publisher, with his most impressive and benevolent air, "we have your welfare at heart. You may write essays and stories and poems as a recreation, or for some future age. But this is the day of the novel, and you are wasting your chance unless you publish one as soon as possible. Touch your novel up, or give it to me as it is. You will certainly make a big thing out of it."

"Perhaps," said the young Man of Letters, thoughtfully; "but what if I would rather write the things that please me most, and try to do good work?"

My Uncle Peter looked at him half-quizzically, yet with a smile of benevolent approval, and conferred upon him the honour and reward of escorting the True Story Teller home in his canoe that evening, across the swirling river, where the molten gold of sunset ran slowly to the sea.

SOME REMARKS ON GULLS

WITH A FOOT-NOTE ON A FISH

SOME REMARKS ON GULLS
WITH A FOOT-NOTE ON A FISH

I

CITY GULLS

THE current estimate of the sea-gull as an intellectual force is compressed into the word "gullibility"—a verbal monument of contempt. But when we think how many things the gull does that we cannot do—how he has mastered the arts of flying and floating, so that he is equally at home in the air and on the water; how cleverly he adapts himself to his environment, keeping warm among the ice-floes in winter and cool when all the rest of the folks at the summer watering-places are sweltering in the heat; how well he holds his own against the encroachments of that grasping animal, man, who has driven so many other wild creatures to the wall, and over it into extinction; how prudently he accepts and utilizes all the devices of civilization which suit him, (such as steamship-lanes across the Atlantic, and dumping-scows in city harbors, and fish-oil factories on the sea-

215

shore), without becoming in the least civilized himself—in short, when we consider how he succeeds in doing what every wise person is trying to do, living his own proper life amid various and changing circumstances, it seems as if we might well reform the spelling of that supercilious word, and write it "gull-ability."

But probably the gull would show no more relish for the compliment than he has hitherto shown distaste for the innuendo; both of them being inedible, and he of a happy disposition, indifferent to purely academic opinions of his rank and station in the universe. Imagine a gull being disquieted because some naturalist solemnly averred that a hawk or a swallow was a better master of the art of flight; or a mocking-bird falling into a mood of fierce resentment or nervous depression because some professor of music declared that the hermit thrush had a more spontaneous and inspired song! The gull goes a-flying in his own way and the mocking-bird sits a-singing his roundelay, original or imitated, just as it comes to him; and neither of them is angry or depressed when a critic makes odious comparisons, because they are both doing the best that they know with "a whole and happy heart." Not so with poets, orators, opera-singers, and other human professors of

216

the high-flying and cantatory arts. They are often perturbed and acerbated, and sometimes diverted from their proper course by the winds of adverse comment.

When Cicero Tomlinson began his career as a public speaker he showed a very pretty vein of humour, which served to open his hearer's minds with honest laughter to receive his plain and forcible arguments. But someone remarked that his speaking lacked dignity and weight; so he loaded himself with the works of Edmund Burke; and now he discusses the smallest subject with a ponderosity suited to the largest. The charm of Alfred Tennyson Starling's early lyrics was unmistakable. But in an evil day a newspaper announced that his poetry smelled of the lamp and was deficient in virility. Alfred took it painfully to heart, and fell into a violent state of Whitmania. Have you seen his patient imitations of the long-lined, tumultuous one?

After all, the surest way to be artificial is to try to be natural according to some other man's recipe.

One reason why the wild children of nature attract our eyes, and give us an inward, subtle satisfaction in watching them, is because they seem so confident that their own way of doing things is, for them at least, the best way. They let themselves go, on the air, in the water, over the hills, among the trees, and do not ask for admiration or correction from people who are differently built. The sea-gulls flying over a busy port of commerce, or floating at ease on the discoloured, choppy, churned-up waves of some great river,

> *"Bordered by cities, and hoarse*
> *With a thousand cries,"*

are unconscious symbols of nature's self-reliance and content with her ancient methods. Not a whit have they changed their manner of flight, their comfortable, rocking-chair seat upon the water, their creaking, eager voice of hunger and excitement, since the days when the port was a haven of solitude, and the river was crossed only by the red man's canoe passing from forest to forest. They are untroubled by the fluctuations of trade, the calms and tempests which afflict the stock market, the hot waves and cold waves of politics. They do not fash themselves about the fashions—except, perhaps, that silly and barbarous one of adorning the headgear of women with the remains of dead gulls, which they probably dislike and disapprove. They do not ask whether life is worth living, but launch themselves boldly upon the supposition that it is, and seem to find it interesting, various, and highly enjoyable, even among wharves, steamboats, and factory chimneys.

My first acquaintance with these untamed visitors of the metropolis was

"When that I was and a littel tine boy,"

and lived on the Heights of Brooklyn. A nurse, whose hateful official relation was mitigated by many amiable personal qualities—she was a rosy Irish girl—had the happy idea of going with me, now and then, for a "day off" and a breath of fresh air, on one of the ferry-boats that ply the waters of Manhattan. Sometimes she took one of the ordinary ferries that went straight over to New York and back again; but more often she chose a boat that proposed a longer and more adventurous voyage—to Hoboken, or Hunter's Point, or Staten Island. We would make the trip to and fro several times, but Biddy never paid, so far as my memory goes, more than one fare. By what arrangement or influence she made the deck-hands considerately blind to this repetition of the journey without money and without price, I neither knew nor cared, being altogether engaged with playing about the deck and admiring the wonders of the vasty deep.

219

The other boats were wonderful, especially the big sailing-ships, which were far more numerous then than they are now. The steam tugs, with their bluff, pushing, hasty manners, were very attractive, and I wondered why all of them had a gilt eagle, instead of a gull, on top of the wheel-house. A little rowboat, tossing along the edge of the wharves, or pushing out bravely for Governor's Island, seemed to be full of perilous adventure. But most wonderful of all were the sea-gulls, flying and floating all over the East River and the North River and the bay.

Where did they come from? It was easy to see where they got their living; they were "snappers-up of unconsidered trifles" from every passing vessel whose cabin-boy threw the rubbish overboard. If you could succeed in getting off the peel of an orange in two or three big pieces, or if you could persuade yourself to leave a reasonably large core of an apple, or, best of all, if you had the limp skin of a yellow banana, you cast the forbidden fruit into the water, and saw how quickly one of the gulls would pick it up, and how beautifully the others would fight him for it. Evidently gulls have a wider range of diet than little boys; also they have never been told that it is wrong to fight.

220

SOME REMARKS ON GULLS

"How greedy they are! What makes some
of them white and some of them gray? They
must be different kinds; or else the gray ones
are the father and mother gulls. But if that is
so, it is funny that the white ones are the best
fliers and seem able to take things away from
the gray ones. How would you like to fly like
that? They swoop around and go just where
they want to. Perhaps that is the way the
angels fly; only of course the angels are much
larger, and very much more particular about
what they eat. Isn't it queer that all the gulls
have eyes just alike—black and shiny and
round, just like little shoe-buttons? How fun-
nily they swim! They sit right down on the
water as if it wasn't wet. Don't you wish you
could do that? Look how they tuck up their
pinky feet under them when they fly, and how
they turn their heads from side to side, looking
for something good to eat. See, there's a great
big flock all together in the water, over yonder,
must be a thousand hundred. Now they all
fly up at once, like when you tear a newspaper
into little scraps and throw a handful out of
the window. Where do you suppose they go at
night? Perhaps they sleep on the water. That
must be fun! Do they have gulls in Ireland,
Biddy, and are all their eyes black and shiny?"

"Sure!" says Biddy. "An' they do be a hundred toimes bigger an' foiner than these wans. The feathers o' thim shoines in the sun loike silver and gowld, an' their oyes is loike jools, an' they do be floying fasther than the ships can sail. If ye was only seein' some o' thim rale Oirish gulls, ye'd think no more o' these little wans!"

This increases your determination to go to the marvellous green island some day; but it does not in the least diminish your admiration for the gulls of Manhattan. In the summer, when you go to the seaside and watch the

"Gray spirits of the sea and of the shore"

sailing over the white beach or floating on the blue waves of the unsullied ocean, you wonder whether these country gulls are happier than the city gulls. That they are different you are sure, and also that they must have less variety in their diet, hardly any banana-skins and orange-peel at all. But then they have more fish, and probably more fun in catching them.

These are memories of old times—the ancient days before the Great Invasion of the English Sparrows—the good old days when orioles and robins still built their nests in Brooklyn trees, and Brooklyn streets still resounded to the

222

SOME REMARKS ON GULLS

musical cries of the hucksters: "Radishees! *noo* radishees!" or "Ole clo' an' bottles! any *ole* clo' to sell!" or "Shad O! *fre-e-sh* shad!" In that golden age we played football around the old farmhouse on Montague Terrace, coasted down the hill to Fulton Ferry, and made an occasional expedition to Manhattan to observe the strange wigwams and wild goats of the tribe of squatters who inhabited the rocky country south of the newly discovered Central Park. *Eheu fugaces!*

There was a long interval of years after that when the sea-gulls of the harbour did not especially interest me. But now again, of late, I have begun to find delight in them. Conscience, awakened by responsibility, no longer permits those surreptitiously repeated voyages without a repeated fare. But I go through the gate at the end of each voyage, and consider twelve cents a reasonable price for the pleasure of travelling up and down the North River for an hour and watching the city gulls in their winter holiday.

I know a little more about them now. They are almost all herring gulls, although occasionally a stray bird of another species may be seen. The dark-gray ones are the young. They grow lighter and more innocent-looking as they grow older, until they are pure white, except the back

and the top of the wings, which are of the soft-
est pearl gray.   The head and neck, in winter,
are delicately pencilled with dusky lines.   The
bill is bright yellow and rather long, with the
upper part curved and slightly hooked, for a
good hold on slippery little fish.   The foot has
three long toes in front and a foolish little short
one behind.   The web between the front toes
goes down to the tips; but it makes only a small
paddle, after all, and when it comes to swimming, the loon and the duck and several other
birds can easily distance the gull.   It is as a
floater that he excels in water sports; he rides
the waves more lightly and gracefully than any
other creature.

> "*The gull, high floating like a sloop unladen,*
> *Lets the loose water waft him as it will;*
> *The duck, round-breasted as a rustic maiden,*
> *Paddles and plunges, busy, busy, still.*"

But it is when the gull rises into the air,
where, indeed, he seems to spend most of his
time, that you perceive the perfection of his
design as a master of motion.   The spread of
his wings is more than twice the length of his
body, and every feather of those long, silvery-
pearly, crescent fans seems instinct with the
passion and the skill of flight.   He rises and

falls without an effort; he swings and turns from side to side with balancing motions like a skater; he hangs suspended in the air immovable as if he were held there by some secret force of levitation; he dives suddenly head foremost and skims along the water, feet dangling and wings flapping, to snatch a bit of food from the surface with his crooked golden bill. If the morsel is too large for him to swallow, look how quickly three or four other gulls will follow him, trying to take it away. How he turns and twists and dodges, and how cleverly they head him off and hang on his airy trail, like winged hounds, giving tongue with thin and querulous voices, half laughing and half crying and altogether hungry. He cannot say a word, for his mouth is full. He gulps hastily at his booty, trying to get it down before the others catch him. But it is too big for his gullet, and he drops it in the very act and article of happy deglutition. The largest and whitest of his pursuers scoops up the morsel almost before it touches the waves, and flaps away to enjoy his piratical success in some quiet retreat.

What a variety of cooking the gulls enjoy from the steamships and sailing-vessels of various nationalities which visit Manhattan ! French cooks, Italian, German, Spanish, English, Swedish—cooks of all races minister to their appetites. Whenever a panful of scraps is thrown out from the galley, a flock of gulls may be seen fluttering over their fluent *table d'hôte*. Their shrill, quavering cries of joy and expectancy sound as if the machinery of their emotions were worked by rusty pulleys; their sharp eyes glisten, and their great wings flap and whirl together in a confusion of white and gray. It is said that they do useful service as scavengers of the harbor. No doubt; but to me they comment themselves chiefly as visible embodiments and revelations of the mystery, wonder, and gladness of flight.

What do we know about it, after all? We call this long-winged fellow *Larus argentatus smithsonianus*. We find that his normal temperature is about two degrees higher than ours, and that he breathes faster, and that his bones are lighter, and that his body is full of air-sacs, fitting him to fly. But how does he do it? How does he poise himself on an invisible ledge of air,

"*Motionless as a cloud* . . .
*That heareth not the loud winds when they call,
And moveth altogether if it move at all?*"

How does he sail after a ship, with wings outspread, against the wind, never seeming to move a feather? You understand how a kite mounts upon the breeze: the string holds it from going back, so it must go up. But where is the string that holds the gull?

I like these city gulls because they come to us in winter, when the gypsy part of our nature is most in need of comforting reminders that the world is not yet entirely dead or civilized. A man that I know once wrote a poem about them, and sent it to a magazine. It was evidently an out-of-door poem and so the editor put it in the midsummer number,—when you might cross the ferry a hundred times without seeing a single gull. They do not begin to come to town until October; and it is well on into November before their social season begins. In March and April they begin to flit again, and by May they are all away northward, to the inland lakes among the mountains, or to the rocky islands of the Maine coast. Let us follow them.

II

A GULL PARADISE

In the waters south of Cape Cod, where bluefish and other gamy surface swimmers are found, the gulls are often useful guides to the fisherman. When he sees a great flock of them flut-

tering over the water, he suspects that the objects of his pursuit are there, feeding from below
on the squid, the shiners, or the skip-jack, on
which the gulls are feeding from above. So the
fisherman sails as fast as possible in that direction, wishing to drag his trolls through the
school of fish while they are still hungry. But
in the colder waters around the island of Mount
Desert, where the blue-fish have never come
and the mackerel have gone away, the sign of
the fluttering gulls does not indicate fish to be
caught, but fish which have already been caught,
and which some other fisherman is cleaning for
the market as he hurries home. The gulls follow his boat and glean from the waves behind it.
They are commentators now, not prophets.

In these blue and frigid deeps the real sport
of angling is unknown. There is instead a
rather childish, but amusing, game of salt-water
grab-bag. You let down a heavy lump of lead
and two big hooks baited with clams into thirty,
forty, or sixty feet of water. Then you wait
until something nudges the line. Then you give
the line a quick jerk, and pull in, hand over
hand, and see what you have drawn from the
grab-bag. It may be a silly, but nutritious
cod, gaping in surprise at this curious termina-
tion of his involuntary rise in the world; or a

silvery haddock, staring at you with round, reproachful eyes; or a pollock, handsome but worthless; or a shiny, writhing dog-fish, whose villainy is written in every line of his degenerate, chinless face. It may be that spiny gargoyle of the sea, a sculpin; or a soft and stupid hake from the mud-flats. It may be any one of the grotesque products of Neptune's vegetable garden, a sea-cucumber, a sea-carrot, or a sea-cabbage. Or it may be nothing at all. When you have made your grab, and deposited the result, if it be edible, in the barrel which stands in the middle of the boat, you try another grab, and that's the whole story.

It is astonishing how much amusement apparently sane men can get out of such a simple game as this. The interest lies, first, in the united effort to fill the barrel, and second, in the rivalry among the fishermen as to which of them shall take in the largest cod or the greatest number of haddock, these being regarded as prize packages. The sculpin and the sea vegetables may be compared to comic valentines, which expose the recipient to ridicule. The dog-fish are like tax notices and assessments; the man who gets one of them gets less than nothing, for they count against the catcher. It is quite as much a game of chance as politics or poker. You do not know on which side of the boat the good fish are hidden. You cannot tell the difference between the nibble of a cod and the bite of a dog-fish. You have no idea what is coming to you, until you have hauled in almost all of your line and caught sight of your allotment wriggling and whirling in the blue water. Sometimes you get twins.

The barrel is nearly full. Let us stop fishing and drifting. Hoist the jib, and trim in the main-sheet. The boat ceases to rock lazily on the tide. The life of the wind enters into her, and she begins to step over the waves and to cut through them, sending bright showers of spray from her bow, and leaving a swirling, bubbling, foaming wake astern. Were there ever waters so blue, or woods so green, or rocky shores so boldly and variously cut, or mountains so clear in outline and so jewel-like in shifting colours, as these of Mount Desert? Was there ever an air which held a stronger, sweeter cordial, fragrant with blended odours of the forest and the sea, soothing, exhilarating, and life-renewing?

Here is the place to see it all, and to drain the full cup of delight; not a standpoint, but a sailing-line just beyond Baker's Island: a voyager's field of vision, shifting, changing, unfolding, as new bays and islands come into view, and new peaks arise, and new valleys open in the line of emerald and amethyst and carnelian and tourmaline hills. You can count all the summits: Newport, and Green, and Pemetic, and Sargent, and Brown, and Dog, and Western. The lesser hills, the Bubbles, Bald Mountain, Flying Mountain, and the rest, detach themselves one after another and stand out from their background of green and gray. How rosy the cliffs of Otter and Seal Harbor glow in the sunlight! How magically the great white flower of foam expands and closes on the sapphire water as the long waves, one by one, pass over the top of the big rock between us and Islesford! This is a bird's-eye view: not a high-flying bird, circling away up in the sky, or perched upon some lofty crag, as Tennyson describes the eagle:—

"Close to the sun in lonely lands,
Ringed with the azure world he stands;
The wrinkled sea beneath him crawls,
He watches from his mountain-walls;"

but a to-and-fro-travelling bird, keeping close to sea and shore. It is a gull's-eye view—just as the flocks of herring gulls see it every day, passing back and forth from their seaward nesting-

place to their favourite feeding-ground at Bar
Harbor. There they go now, flapping southward with the breeze. We will go with them to
their island home, and eat our dinner while
they are digesting theirs.

Great and Little Duck Islands lie about ten
miles off shore from Seal Harbor. Their name
suggests that they were once the haunt of various kinds of sea-fowl. But the ducks have been
almost, if not quite, exterminated; and the herring gulls would probably have gone the same
way, but for the exertions of the Audubon Society, which have resulted in the reservation of
the islands as a breeding-ground under govern-
mental protection. It has taken a long time
to awaken the American people to the fact that
the wild and beautiful creatures of earth and
air and sea are a precious part of the common
inheritance, and that their needless and heed-
less destruction, by pot-hunters or plume-hunt-
ers or silly shooters who are not happy unless
they are destroying something, is a crime against
the commonwealth which must be punished or
prevented. The people are not yet wide awake,
but they are beginning to get their eyes open;
and the State of Maine, which was once the
Butchers' Happy Hunting Ground, is now a
leader in the enactment and enforcement of
good game laws.

SOME REMARKS ON GULLS

There is only one place on the shore of Great
Duck where you can land comfortably when
the wind has any northing in it, and that is a
little cove among the rocks, below a fisherman's
shanty, on the lower end of the island. Here
there are a few cleared acres; some low stone
walls dividing abandoned fields; the cellar of a
vanished house, and a ruined fireplace and chimney; a little enclosure, overgrown with bushes
and weeds, marking a lonely, forgotten burial-
ground.

There are few gulls to be seen at this end of
the island; it is a tranquil, forsaken place where
we can sit beside our fire of driftwood and eat
our broiled fish and bread, and smoke an after-
dinner pipe of peace. A grassy foot-path leads
down the fields, and across a salt-meadow, and
along a high sea-wall of rocks and pebbles cast
up by the storms, and so by a rude wood-road
through a forest of spruce-trees to the higher
part of the island. It rises perhaps a hundred
feet or more above the sea, with a steep shore
built of huge sloping ledges of flat rock. On the
seaward point is the light-house, with the three
dwelling-houses of the keepers, all precisely
alike, immaculately neat and trim, surrounded
by a long picket fence, and presenting a front of
indomitable human order and discipline to the
tumultuous and unruly ocean, which heaves

away untamed and unbroken to the shores of
Spain and Brittany.

The chief keeper of the light, Captain Stanley,
who has been with it since it was first kindled
twenty years ago, is also the warden of the sea-
gulls. All around us, in the air, on the green
slopes of the island, on the broad gray granite
ledges, on the dancing blue waves, his feathered
flocks are scattered, and their innumerable
laughter and shrill screaming confuse the ear.
The spruce-trees on the top of the island and
the eastward slopes are almost all dead; their
fallen trunks and branches and upturned roots
cover the little hillocks and hollows in all directions. The gulls' nests are hidden away among
this gray *débris*, or in crevices among the rocks
sheltered as much as possible from the wind,
and the rain.

They are not very wonderful from an architectural point of view, being nothing more than
rough little circles of dried twigs and grass mat-
ted together, with perhaps a bit of seaweed or
moss for padding in the case of a parent with
luxurious tastes. Three eggs in a nest is the
rule, and all that the average mother-gull wants
is a place where she can hold them together and
keep them warm until they are hatched. The
young birds are præcocial; they emerge from

the shell with a full suit of downy feathers, and are able to walk after a fashion, and to swim pretty well, almost from the day of their second and completed birth. The young of altricial birds, like orioles, and bluebirds, and thrushes, being born naked and helpless, have a reason for loving their nest-homes, so carefully and delicately built to shelter their nude infancy. But the young gull cares not for "a local habitation and a name." All that he wants of home is a father and mother, nimble and assiduous in bringing food to him while he flops around, practising his legs and his wings.

It is August now, and the eggs are gone, shells and all. Almost all of the young gulls are accomplished swimmers and fair fliers by this time, and I suppose the majority of the brood can go with their parents to the nearer harbours and along the island shores to forage for themselves. But there are a few backward or lazy children—perhaps a hundred—still hanging around the places where they chipped the egg, hiding among the roots of the trees or crouching beside the rocks. What quaint, ungainly creatures they are! Big-headed, awkward, dusky, like gnomes or goblins, they hop and scuffle away as you come near them, stumbling over the tangled dead branches and the tussocks of

235

grass, with outspread wings and clumsy motions. Follow one a little while and he will take refuge in a hole under a fallen tree, or between two big stones, squatting there without much apparent fright while you pat his back or gently scratch his head. But you must be careful not to follow the youngsters who are near the edge of the sea when there is a surf running, for if you alarm them they will plunge into the water and be bruised and wounded, perhaps killed, by the breakers throwing them against the rocks.

Wild animals, like polecats and minks, who would be likely to prey upon the young birds, are not allowed to reside on the island; and it is too far to swim from the mainland. But I wonder why large hawks and other birds of prey do not resort to this place as a marine restaurant. Perhaps a young gull is too big, or too tough, or too high-flavoured a dish for them. Possibly the old gulls know how to fight for their offspring. I suppose that enough of the adult birds are always on hand for defence, although during a good part of the day the majority of the flock are away at the feeding-grounds.

I opened the gate of the light-house enclosure and went in. Three little children who were playing in the garden came shyly up to me, each silently offering a flower. The keeper of the light, who is a most intelligent man and an ardent Audubonite, asked me into his sitting-room and told me a lot about his gulls.

In the spring, the first of them come back in March, sometimes arriving in a snowstorm. They keep to the shore most of the time, but fuss around a little, pulling old nests to pieces or making new ones. About the first of May, they move up to the centre of the island. There are three or four thousand of them, and not quite half as many nests. By the middle of May the first egg may be expected, and in the second week of June the first gray chick puts out his big head. A week later the brood is all hatched and the parental troubles begin.

"The old birds," says Mr. Stanley, "do not fail to provide food for their young, although as the birds get large the old ones have to go some-times many miles to do it, but, as a general thing, there is plenty for them. I have watched them coming back at night, appearing very tired, flying very low, one behind the other. They would light near where the young should be and call, and the chicks would rush up to the old bird and pick its bill; after the proper time the old bird will stretch out its neck, and up will come a mess of almost everything, from bread to sea-cucumbers, livers, fish (all the small kind). If there is anything left after the feast the old bird will swallow it again. Woe betide the young bird that belongs to a neighbour, who tries to fill up at the wrong place! I have seen a young bird killed by one blow from the old bird's bill, his head torn in two. As the young birds grow, the old birds bring them larger fish to swallow. We have a few old birds who know the time we feed our hens, and when that time draws near they are on hand to dine with the hens."

By the latter part of August, having done their duties, the old birds, the white ones, begin to leave the island. The dingy youngsters are slower to forsake their Eden of innocence, lingering on beside the unsullied waters and beneath the crystalline skies until the frosts of late September warn them that winter is at hand. Then the last of the colony take flight, winging their way southward leisurely and comfortably, putting in at many a port where fish are cleaned and scraps are thrown overboard, until they arrive at their chosen harbour by some populous and smoke-clouded city, and learn to dodge the steamboats and swim in troubled waters.

So the Gull Paradise is deserted by all but its

guardians. The school district of Duck Island
—the smallest in the United States—resumes
its activities; the school-house is open, the
teacher raps on the desk, and the fourteen children of the keepers apply themselves to the
knowledge that is dried in books.

III

IN THE GULLS' BATH-TUB

Over our cottage we saw them flying inland
every morning about ten or eleven o'clock; in
groups of three or four; in companies of twelve
or twenty; sometimes a solitary bird, hurrying
a little as if he were belated. Over our cottage
we saw them flying seaward every afternoon,
one or two at a time, and then, at last, a larger
company all together. The trail through the
woods, up along the lovely mountain-brook,
led us in the same direction as the gulls' path
through the air. A couple of miles of walking
underneath green boughs brought us to the
shores of Jordan Pond, lying in a deep gorge
between the mountains of rock with the rounded,
forest-clad Bubbles at its head, and the birches,
and maples, and poplars, and hemlocks fringing
its clean, stony shores. Then we understood
what brought the gulls up from the sea every

day. They came for a fresh-water bath and a little fun in the woods.

Look at them, gathered like a flotilla, in the centre of the pond. They are not feeding; they are not attending to any business of importance; they are not even worrying about their young; they are not doing anything at all but "bathing" themselves, as my little lad used to say, in this clear, cool, unsalted water, and having the best time in the world. See how they swim lazily this way or that way, as the fancy strikes them. See how they duck their heads, and stretch their long wings in the air, and splash the water over one another; how they preen their feathers and rise on the surface, shaking themselves. Here comes a trio of late starters, flying up from the sea. They hover overhead a moment, crying out to the crowd below, which answers them with a general shout and a flutter of excitement. Didn't you hear what they said?

"Hello, fellows! How's the water?"

"Bully! Just right—come in quick's you can!" So the new arrivals swoop down, spreading out their tails like fans, and dangling their feet under them, and settling in the centre of the crowd amid general hilarity.

How long the gulls stay at their bath I do

not know. Probably some of the busy and con-
scientious ones just hurry in for a dip and hurry
back again. Others, of a more pleasure-loving
temperament, make the trip more than once,
like a boy I knew, whose proud boast it was
that he had gone in swimming seven times in
one afternoon. The very idle and self-indulgent
ones, I reckon, spend nearly the whole day in
their spacious and well-fitted bath-tub.

The mountain lake has been turned into a
reservoir for the neighbouring village of Seal
Harbor. But the gulls do not know that, I am
sure; nor would anyone else who judged by
outward appearances suspect that such a trans-
formation had taken place. For the dam at
the outlet is made of rough stones, very low,
almost unnoticeable; and the water has not
been raised enough to kill any of the trees or
spoil the shore. Jordan Pond, which was named
for a commonplace lumberman who used to
cut timber on its banks, and which has, so far
as I know, no tradition or legend of any kind
connected with it, is still as wild, as lovely, as
perfect in its lonely charm as if it were consecrated and set apart to the memory of a score
of old romances.

At the lower end, in an open space of slightly
rising ground, there is an ancient farmhouse

which has been extended and piazzaed and made into a rustic place of entertainment. Here the fashionable summer-folk of the various harbours come to drink afternoon tea and to eat famous dinners of broiled chicken, baked potatoes, and pop-overs. The proprietor has learned from the modern author and advertiser the secret of success; avoid versatility and stick to the line in which the public know you. Having won a reputation on pop-overs and chickens, he continues to turn them out with diligence and fidelity, like short-stories of a standard pattern.

I asked him if there was any fishing in the lake. He said that there was plenty of fishing; but he said it in a tone which made me doubtful about his meaning. "What kind of fish were there?" "Trout by nature, and landlocked salmon by artificial planting." "Could we fish for them?" "Sure; but as for catching anything big enough to keep—well, he did not want to encourage us. It was two or three years since any good fish had been caught in the lake, though there had been plenty of fishing. But in old times men used to come over from Hull's Cove, fishing through the ice, and they caught"—then followed the usual piscatorial legends of antiquity.

But the Gypsy girl and I were not to be disheartened by historical comparisons. We insisted on putting our living luck to the proof, and finding out for ourselves what kind of fish were left in Jordan Pond. We had a couple of four-ounce rods, one of which I fitted up with a troll, while she took the oars in a round-bottomed, snub-nosed white boat, and rowed me slowly around the shore. The water was very clear; at a depth of twenty feet we could see every stone and stick on the bottom—and no fish! We tried a little farther out, where the water was deeper. My guide was a merry rower and the voyage was delightful, but we caught nothing.

Let us set up the other rod, while we are trolling, and try a few casts with the fly as we move along. I will put the trolling-rod behind me, leaning over the back-board; if a fish should strike, he would hook himself and I could pick up the rod and land him. Now we will straighten out a leader and choose some flies—a silver doctor and a queen of the water—how would those do? Or perhaps a royal coachman would be——Chrrr-p! goes the reel. I turn hastily around, just in time to see the trolling-rod vanish over the stern of the boat. Stop, stop! Back water—hard as you can! Too late! There goes my best-beloved little rod, with a reel and fifty yards of line, settling down in the deep water, almost out of sight, and slowly following the flight of that invisible fish, who has hooked himself and my property at the same time.

This is a piece of bad luck. Shall we let the day end with this? "Never," says the Gypsy. "Adventures ought to be continued till they end with good luck. We will put a long line on the other rod, and try that beautiful little phantom minnow, the silver silk one that came from Scotland. There must be some good fish in the pond, since they are big enough to run away with your tackle."

Round and round the shore she rows, past the points of broken rocks, underneath the rugged bluffs, skirting all the shelving bays. Faintly falls the evening breeze, and behind the western ridge of Jordan Mountain suddenly the sun drops down. Look, the gulls have all gone home. Creeping up the rosy side of Pemetic, see old Jordan's silhouette sketched in shadow by the sun. Hark, was that a coaching horn, sounding up from Wildwood Road? There's the whistle of the boat coming round the point at Seal. How it sinks into the silence, fading gradually away. Twilight settles slowly down, all around the wooded shore, and across the opal lake——

Chr-r-r-r! sings the reel. The line tightens.

SOME REMARKS ON GULLS

The little rod, firmly gripped in my hand, bends into a bow of beauty, and a hundred feet behind us a splendid silver salmon leaps into the air. "What is it?" cries the Gypsy, "a fish?" It is a fish, indeed, a noble ouananiche, and well hooked. Now if the gulls were here, who grab little fish suddenly and never give them a chance, or if the mealy-mouthed sentimentalists were here, who like their fish slowly strangled to death in nets, they should see a fairer method of angling.

The weight of the fish is twenty times that of the rod against which he matches himself. The tiny hook is caught painlessly in the gristle of his jaw. The line is long and light. He has the whole lake to play in, and he uses almost all of it, running, leaping, sounding the deep water, turning suddenly to get a slack line. The Gypsy, tremendously excited, manages the boat with perfect skill, rowing this way and that way, advancing or backing water to meet the tactics of the fish, and doing the most important part of the work.

After half an hour the ouananiche begins to grow tired and can be reeled in near to the boat. We can see him distinctly as he gleams in the dark water. It is time to think of landing him. Then we remember, with a flash of despair, that we have no landing-net! To lift him from the water by the line would break it in an instant. There is not a foot of the rocky shore smooth enough to beach him on. Our caps are far too small to use as a net for such a fish. What to do? We must row around with him gently and quietly for another ten minutes until he is quite weary and tame. Now let me draw him softly in toward the boat, slip my fingers under his gills to get a firm hold, and lift him quickly over the gunwale before he can gasp or kick. A tap on the head with the empty rod-case—there he is—the prettiest landlocked salmon that I ever saw, plump, round, perfectly shaped and coloured, and just six and a half pounds in weight, the record fish of Jordan Pond!

Do you think that the Gypsy and I wept over our lost rod, or were ashamed of our flannel shirts and tweeds, as we sat down to our broiled chickens and pop-overs that evening, on the piazza of the tea-house, among the white frocks and Tuxedo jackets of the diners-out? No, for there was our prize lying in state on the floor beside our table. "And we caught him," said she, "in the gulls' bath-tub!"

LEVIATHAN

LEVIATHAN

THE village of Samaria in the central part of
the State of Connecticut resembled the
royal city of Israel, after which it was named,
in one point only. It was perched upon the
top of a hill, encircled by gentle valleys which
divided it from an outer ring of hills still more
elevated, almost mountainous. But, except this
position in the centre of the stage, you would
find nothing theatrical or striking about the
little New England hill-town: no ivory palaces
to draw down the denunciations of a minor
prophet, no street of colonnades to girdle the
green eminence with its shining pillars, not even
a dirty picturesqueness such as now distin-
guishes the forlorn remnant of the once haughty
city of Omri and of Herod.

Neat, proper, reserved, not to say conventional, the Connecticut Samaria concealed its
somewhat chilly architectural beauties beneath
a veil of feathery elms and round-topped maples. It was not until you had climbed the hill
from the clump of houses and shops which had
grown up around the railway station,—a place

of prosperous ugliness and unabashed modernity, —that you perceived the respectable evidences of what is called in America "an ancient town." The village green, and perhaps a half dozen of the white wooden houses which fronted it with their prim porticoes, were more than a hundred years old. The low farmhouse, which showed its gambrel-roof and square brick chimney a few rods down the northern road, was a relic of colonial days. The stiff white edifice with its pointed steeple, called in irreverent modern phrase the "Congo" church, claimed an equal antiquity; but it had been so often repaired and "improved" to suit the taste of various epochs, that the traces of Sir Christopher Wren in its architecture were quite confused by the admixture of what one might describe as the English Sparrow style.

The other buildings on the green, or within sight of it along the roads north, south, east, and west, had been erected or built-over at different periods, by prosperous inhabitants or returning natives who wished to have a summer cottage in their birth-place. These structures, though irreproachable in their moral aspect, indicated that the development of the builder's art in Samaria had not followed any known historical scheme, but had been conducted along sporadic lines of imitation, and interrupted at least once by a volcanic outbreak of the style named, for some inscrutable reason, after Queen Anne. On the edges of the hill, looking off in various directions over the encircling vale, and commanding charming views of the rolling ridges which lay beyond, were the houses of the little summer colony of artists, doctors, lawyers, and merchants. Two or three were flamboyant, but for the most part they blended rather gently with the landscape, and were of a modesty which gave their owners just ground for pride.

The countenance of the place was placid. It breathed an air of repose and satisfaction, a spirit which when it refers to outward circumstances is called contentment, and when it refers to oneself is called complacency. The Samaritans, in fact, did not think ill of themselves, and of their village they thought exceedingly well. There was nothing in its situation, its looks, its customs which they would have wished to alter; and when a slight change came, a new house, a pathway on the other side of the green, an iron fence around the graveyard, golf-links in addition to the tennis-courts, a bridge-whist afternoon to supplement the croquet club, by an unconscious convention its novelty was swiftly eliminated and in a short time it became one of the "old traditions." Decidedly a place of peace was Samaria in Connecticut,—a place in which "the struggle for life" and the rivalries and contests of the great outside world were known only by report. Yet, being human, it had its own inward strifes; and of one of these I wish to tell the tale.

In the end this internal conflict centred about Leviathan; but in the beginning I believe it was of an ecclesiastical nature. At all events it did not run its course without a manifest admixture of the *odium theologicum,* and it came near to imperilling the cause of Christian unity in Samaria.

The Episcopal Church was really one of the more recent old institutions of the village. It stood beside the graveyard, just around the corner from the village green; and the type of its wooden architecture, which was profoundly early Gothic and was painted of a burnt-umber hue sprinkled with sand to imitate brownstone, indicated that it must have been built in the Upjohn Period, about the middle of the nineteenth century. But Samaria, without the slightest disloyalty to the principles of the Puritans, had promptly adopted and assimilated the Episcopal form of worship. The singing by a voluntary quartette of mixed voices, the hours of service, even the sermons, were all of the Samaritan type. The old rector, Dr. Snodgrass, a comfortably stout and evangelical man, lived for forty years on terms of affectionate intimacy with three successive ministers of the Congregational Church, the deacons of which shared with his vestrymen the control of the village councils.

The summer residents divided their attendance impartially between the two houses of worship. Even in the distribution of parts in the amateur theatricals which were given every year by the villagers in the town hall at the height of the season, no difference was made between the adherents of the ancient faith of Connecticut and the followers of the more recently introduced order of Episcopacy. When old Dr. Snodgrass died and was buried, the Rev. Cotton Mather Hopkins, who was an energetic widower of perhaps thirty-five years, made an eloquent address at his funeral, comparing him to the prophet Samuel, the apostle John, and a green bay tree whose foundations are built upon the rock. In short, all was tranquil in the ecclesiastical atmosphere of Samaria. There was not a cloud upon the horizon.

The air changed with the arrival of the new rector, the Rev. Willibert Beauchamp Jones,

B.D., from the Divinity School of St. Jerome at Oshkosh. He was a bachelor, not only of divinity but also in the social sense; a plump young man of eight and twenty summers, with an English accent, a low-crowned black felt hat, blue eyes, a cherubic smile, and very high views on liturgics. He was full of the best intentions toward the whole world, a warm advocate of the reunion of Christendom on *his* platform, and a man of sincere enthusiasm who regarded Samaria as a missionary field and was prepared to consecrate his life to it. The only point in which he was not true to the teachings of his professors at St. Jerome's was the celibacy of the parish clergy. Here he held that the tradition of the Greek Church was to be preferred to that of the Roman, and felt in his soul that the priesthood and matrimony were not inconsistent. In fact, he was secretly ambitious to prove their harmony in his own person. He was a very social young man, and firm in his resolution to be kind and agreeable to everybody, even to those who were outside of the true fold.

Mr. Hopkins called on him without delay and was received with cordiality amounting to *empressement.* The two men talked together in the friendliest manner of interests that they

had in common, books, politics, and out-of-door
sports, to which both of them were addicted.
Mr. Jones offered to lend Mr. Hopkins any of
the new books, with which his library was rather
well stocked, and promised to send over the
Pall Mall Review, to which he was a subscriber,
every week. Mr. Hopkins told Mr. Jones the
name of the best washerwoman in the village,
one of his own new parishioners, as it happened,
and proposed to put him up at once for mem-
bership in the Golf Club. In fact the conversation went off most harmoniously.

"It was extraordinarily kind of you to call so
early, my dear fellow," said Jones as he followed
his guest to the door of the little rectory. "I
take it as a mark of Christian brotherhood; and
naturally, as a clergyman, I want to be as
close as possible to every one who is working in
any way for the good of the place where my
parish lies."

"Of course!" answered Hopkins. "That's all
right. I guess you won't have any trouble
about Christian brotherhood in Samaria. Good-
bye till Monday afternoon."

But as he walked across the green, the skirts
of his black frock-coat flapping in the September breeze, and his brown Fedora hat set at a
reflective angle on the back of his head, he pon-

dered a little over the precise significance of his
confrère's last remark, which had not altogether
pleased him. Was there a subtle shade of difference between those who were working "in
any way" for the good of Samaria, and the
"clergyman" who felt bound to be on good
terms with them?

On Monday afternoon they had appointed to
take a country walk together, and Hopkins,
who was a lean, long-legged, wiry fellow, with
a deep chest, gray eyes, and a short, crisp brown
beard and moustache, led the way at a lively
pace over hill and dale around Lake Marapaug
and back,—fourteen miles in three hours. Jones
was rather red when they returned to the front
gate of the rectory about five o'clock, and he
wiped his beaded forehead with his handkerchief
as he invited his comrade to come in and have
a cup of tea.

"No, thank you," said Hopkins, "I'm just
ready for a bit of work in my study, now. Nice
little stroll, wasn't it? I want you to know the
country about here, and the people too. You
mustn't feel strange in this Puritan region where
my church has been established so long. We'll
soon make you feel at home. Good-bye."

An hour later, when Jones had sipped his tea,
he looked up from an article in the *Pall Mall
Review* and began to wonder whether Hopkins

had meant anything in particular by that last remark.

"He's an awfully good chap, to be sure, but just a bit set in his way. I fancy he has some odd notions. Well, perhaps I shall be able to put him right, if I am patient and friendly. It is rather plain that I shall have a lot of missionary work to do here among these dissenters."

So he turned to his bookshelves and took down a volume on *The Primitive Diaconate and the Reconstruction of Christendom*. Meantime Hopkins was in his study making notes for a series of sermons on "The Scriptural Polity of the Early New England Churches."

Well, you can see from this how the great Leviathan conflict began. Two men meeting with good intentions, both anxious, even determined, to be the best of friends, yet each unconsciously pressing upon the other the only point of difference between them. Now add to this a pair of consciences aggravated by the sense of official responsibilities, and a number of ladies who were alike in cherishing for one or the other of these two men a warm admiration, amounting in several cases, shall I say, to a sentimental adoration, and you have a collection of materials not altogether favourable to a peaceful combination.

My business, however, is with Leviathan, and

therefore I do not propose to narrate the development of the rivalry between these two excellent men. How Mr. Jones introduced an early morning service, and Mr. Hopkins replied with an afternoon musical vespers: how a vested choir of boys was installed in the brown church, and a cornet and a harp appeared in the gallery of the white church: how candles were lighted in the Episcopalian apse, (whereupon Erastus Whipple resigned from the vestry because he said he knew that he was "goin' to act ugly"), and a stereopticon threw illuminated pictures of Palestine upon the wall behind the Congregational pulpit (which induced Abijah Lemon to refuse to pass the plate the next Sunday, because he said he "wa'nt goin' to take up no collection for a peep-show in meetin'"): how a sermon beside the graveyard on "the martyrdom of King Charles I," was followed, on the green, by a discourse on "the treachery of Charles II": how Mrs. Slicer and Mrs. Cutter crossed each other in the transfer of their church relations, because the Slicer boys were not asked to sing in the vested choir, and because Orlando Cutter was displaced as cornetist by a young man from Hitchfield: how the Jonesites learned to speak of themselves as "churchmen" and of their neighbours as "adherents of other religious bodies," while the Hopkinsians politely inquired as to the hours at which "mass was celebrated" in the brown edifice and were careful to speak of their own services as "Divine worship": how Mr. Jones went so far, in his Washington's Birthday Speech, as to compliment the architectural effect of "the old meeting-house on the green, that venerable monument of an earnest period of dissent," to which Mr. Hopkins made the retort courteous by giving thanks, in his prayer on the same occasion, for "the gracious memories of fraternal intercourse which still hallowed the little brown chapel beside the cemetery": how all these strokes and counterstrokes were given and exchanged in a decorous and bloodless religious war which enlivened a Samaritan autumn and winter almost to the point of effervescence: and how they were prevented from doing any great harm by the general good feeling and the constitutional sense of humour of the village, it is not my purpose, I say, to relate in detail.

The fact is, the incipient fermentation passed away almost as naturally and suddenly as it began. Old Cap'n Elihu Gray, who had made a tidy fortune in his voyages to the East Indies and retired to enjoy it in a snug farmhouse beside the Lirrapaug River, a couple of miles below the village, was reputed to be something of a freethinker, but he used to come up, every month, to one or other of the two churches to sample a sermon. His summary of the controversy which threatened the peace of Samaria, seemed to strike the common-sense of his fellow-townsmen in the place where friendly laughter lies.

"Wa'al," said he, puffing a meditative pipe, "I've seen folks pray to cows and jest despise folks 'at prayed to elephants. 'N I've seen folks whose r'ligion wouldn't 'low 'em to eat pig's meat fight with folks whose r'ligion wouldn't 'low 'em to eat meat 't all. But I never seen reel Christians dispise other reel Christians for prayin' at seven in the mornin' 'stead of at eleven, nor yet fight 'bout the difference 'tween a passel o' boys singin' in white nightgowns an' half-a-dozen purty young gals tunin' their voices to a pipe-organ an' a harp o' sollum saound. I don't 'low there is eny devil, but ef ther' wuz, guess that's the kind o' fight 'd make him grin."

This opinion appeared to reach down to the fundamental saving grace of humour in the Samaritan mind. The vestry persuaded the Reverend Willibert that the time was not yet ripe for candles; and the board of deacons in-

duced the Reverend Cotton Mather to substi-
tute a course of lectures on the Women of the
Bible for the stereopticon exhibitions. Hostili-
ties gently frothed themselves away and subsided. Decoration Day was celebrated in Samaria, according to the Hitchfield *Gazette*, "by
a notable gathering in the Town Hall, at which
the Rev. Jones offered an eloquent extempora-
neous prayer and the Rev. Hopkins pronounced
an elegant oration on the Civil War, after which
the survivors partook of a banquet at the Han-
cock Hotel."

But the rivalry between the two leaders, sad
to say, did not entirely disappear with the
peaceful reconciliation and commingling of their
forces. On the contrary, it was as if a general
engagement had been abandoned and both the
opposing companies had resolved themselves
into the happy audience of a single combat. It
was altogether a friendly and chivalrous contest, you understand,—nothing bitter or malicious about it,—but none the less it was a *duel
à l'outrance*, a struggle for the mastery between
two men whom nature had made rivals, and for
whom circumstances had prepared the arena in
the double sphere of love and angling.

Hopkins had become known, during the seven
years of his residence at Samaria, as the best

trout-fisherman of the village, and indeed of all the tributary region. With the black bass there were other men who were his equals, and perhaps one or two, like Judge Ward, who spent the greater part of his summer vacation sitting under an umbrella in a boat on Lake Marapaug, and Jags Witherbee, the village ne'er-do-well, who were his superiors. But with the delicate, speckled, evasive trout he was easily first. He knew all the cold, foaming, musical brooks that sang their way down from the hills. He knew the spring-holes in the Lirrapaug River where the schools of fish assembled in the month of May, waiting to go up the brooks in the warm weather. He knew the secret haunts and lairs of the large fish where they established themselves for the whole season and took toll of the passing minnows. He knew how to let his line run with the current so that it would go in under the bushes without getting entangled, and sink to the bottom of the dark pools, beneath the roots of fallen trees, without the hook catching fast. He knew how to creep up to a stream that had hollowed out a way under the bank of a meadow, without shaking the boggy ground. He had a trick with a detachable float, made from a quill and a tiny piece of cork, that brought him many a fish from the centre of a mill-pond. He knew the best baits for every season,—worms, white grubs, striped minnows, miller's thumbs, bumble-bees, grass-hoppers, young field-mice,—and he knew where to find them.

For it must be confessed that Cotton Mather was a confirmed bait-fisherman. Confession is not the word that he would have used with reference to the fact; he would have called it a declaration of principles, and would have maintained that he was a follower of the best, the most skilful, the most productive, the fairest, the truly Apostolic method of fishing.

Jones, on the other hand, was not a little shocked when he discovered in the course of conversation that his colleague, who was in many respects such a good sportsman, was addicted to fishing with bait. For his own angling education had been acquired in a different school,—among the clear streams of England, the open rivers of Scotland, the carefully preserved waters of Long Island. He had been taught that the artificial fly was the proper lure for a true angler to use.

For coarse fish like perch and pike, a bait was permissible. For middle-class fish, like bass, which would only rise to the fly during a brief and uncertain season, a trolling-spoon or an artificial minnow might be allowed. But for fish whose blood, though cold, was noble,—for gam⌐ fish of undoubted rank like the salmon and the trout, the true angler must use only the lightest possible tackle, the most difficult possible methods, the cleanest and prettiest possible lure,—to wit, the artificial fly. Moreover, he added his opinion that in the long run, taking all sorts of water and weather together, and fishing through the season, a man can take more trout with the fly than with the bait,— that is, of course, if he understands the art of fly-fishing.

You perceive at once that here was a very pretty ground for conflict between the two men, after the ecclesiastical battle had been called off. Their community of zeal as anglers only intensified their radical opposition as to the authoritative and orthodox mode of angling. In the close season, when the practice of their art was forbidden, they discussed its theory with vigour; and many were the wit-combats between these two champions, to which the Samaritans listened in the drug-store-and-post-office that served them in place of a Mermaid Tavern. There was something of Shakspere's quickness and elegance in Willibert's methods; but Cotton Mather had the Jonsonian advantage in learning and in weight of argument.

"It is unhistorical," he said, "to claim that there is only one proper way to catch fish. The facts are against you."

"But surely, my dear fellow," replied Willibert, "there is one best way, and that must be the proper way on which all should unite."

"I don't admit that," said the other, "variety counts for something. Besides, it is up to you to prove that fly-fishing is the best way."

"Well," answered Willibert, "I fancy that would be easy enough. All the authorities are on my side. Doesn't every standard writer on angling say that fly-fishing is the perfection of the art?"

"Not at all," Cotton Mather replied, with some exultation, "Izaak Walton's book is all about bait-fishing, except two or three pages on the artificial fly, which were composed for him by Thomas Barker, a retired confectioner. But suppose all the books were on your side. There are ten thousand men who love fishing and know about fishing, to one who writes about it. The proof of the angler is the full basket."

At this Willibert looked disgusted. "You mistake quantity for quality. It's better to take one fish prettily and fairly than to fill your basket in an inferior way. Would you catch trout with a net?"

Cotton Mather admitted that he would not.

"Well, then, why not carry your discrimination a little farther and reject the coarse bait-hook, and the stiff rod, and the heavy line? Fly-tackle appeals to the æsthetic taste,—the slender, pliant rod with which you land a fish twenty times its weight, the silken line, the gossamer leader, the dainty fly of bright feathers concealing the tiny hook!"

"Concealing!" broke in the advocate of the bait, "that is just the spirit of the whole art of fly-fishing. It's all a deception. The slender rod is made of split cane that will bend double before it breaks; the gossamer leader is of drawn-gut carefully tested to stand a heavier strain than the rod can put upon it. The trout thinks he can smash your tackle, but you know he can't, and you play with him half-an-hour to convince him that you are right. And after all, when you've landed him, he hasn't had even a taste of anything good to eat to console him for being caught,—nothing but a little bunch of feathers which he never would look at if he knew what it was. Don't you think that fly-fishing is something of a piscatorial immorality?"

"Not in the least," answered Willibert, warming to his work, "it is a legitimate appeal, not to the trout's lower instinct, his mere physical hunger, but to his curiosity, his sense of beauty, his desire for knowledge. He takes the fly, not because it looks like an edible insect, for nine times out of ten it doesn't, but because it's pretty and he wants to know what it is. When he has found out, you give him a fair run for his money and bring him to basket with nothing more than a pin-prick in his lip. But what does the bait-fisher do? He deceives the trout into thinking that a certain worm or grub or minnow is wholesome, nourishing, digestible, fit to be swallowed. In that deceptive bait he has hidden a big, heavy hook which sticks deep in the trout's gullet and by means of which the disappointed fish is forcibly and brutally dragged to land. It lacks refinement. It is primitive, violent, barbaric, and so simple that any unskilled village lad can do it as well as you can."

"I think not," said Cotton Mather, now on the defensive, "just let the village-lad try it. Why, the beauty of real bait-fishing is that it requires more skill than any other kind of angling. To present your bait to the wary old trout without frightening him; to make it move in the water so that it shall seem alive and free"; ("deception," murmured Willibert), "to judge the proper moment after he has taken it when you should strike, and how hard; to draw him safely away from the weeds and roots among which he has been lying; all this takes quite a little practice and some skill,—a good deal more, I reckon, than hooking and playing a trout on the clear surface of the water when you can see every motion."

"Ah, there you are," cried Willibert, "that's the charm of fly-fishing! It's all open and above-board. The long, light cast of the fly, 'fine and far off,' the delicate drop of the feathers upon the water, the quick rise of the trout and the sudden gleam of his golden side as he turns, the electric motion of the wrist by which you hook him,—that is the magic of sport."

"Yes," replied the other, "I'll admit there's something in it, but bait-fishing is superior. You take a long pool, late in the season; water low and clear; fish lying in the middle; you can't get near them. You go to the head of the pool in the rapids and stir up the bottom so as to discolour the water a little——"

"Deceptive," interrupted Willibert, "and decidedly immoral!"

"Only a little," continued Cotton Mather, "a very little! Then you go down to the bottom of the pool with a hand-line——"

"A hand-line!" murmured the listener, half-shuddering in feigned horror.

"Yes, a hand-line," the speaker went on firmly, "a long, light hand-line, without a sinker, baited with a single, clean angle-worm, and loosely coiled in your left hand. You cast the hook with your right hand, and it falls lightly without a splash, a hundred feet up stream. Then you pull the line in very gently, just fast enough to keep it from sinking to the bottom. When the trout bites, you strike him and land him by hand, without the help of rod or landing-net or any other mechanical device. Try this once, and you will see whether it is easier than throwing the fly. I reckon this was the way the Apostle Peter fished when he was told to 'go to the sea, and cast a hook, and take up the fish that first cometh up.' It is the only true Apostolic method of fishing."

"But, my dear fellow," answered the other, "the text doesn't say that it was a bait-hook. It may have been a fly-hook. Indeed the text rather implies that, for it speaks of the fish as 'coming up,' and that means rising to the fly."

"Wa'al," said Cap'n Gray, rising slowly and knocking out the ashes of his pipe on the edge of his chair, "I can't express no jedgment on the merits of this debate, seein' I've never been much of a fisher. But ef I wuz, my fust ch'ice'd be to git the fish, an' enny way that got 'em I'd call good."

The arrival of the Springtime, releasing the

streams from their imprisonment of ice, and setting the trout to leaping in every meadow-brook and all along the curving reaches of the swift Lirrapaug, transferred this piscatorial contest from the region of discourse to the region of experiment. The rector proved himself a competitor worthy of the minister's mettle. Although at first he was at some disadvantage on account of his slight acquaintance with the streams, he soon overcame this by diligent study; and while Hopkins did better work on the brooks that were overhung with trees and bushes, Jones was more effective on the open river and in the meadow-streams just at sun-down. They both made some famous baskets that year, and were running neck and neck in the angling field, equal in success.

But in the field of love, I grieve to say, their equality was of another kind. Both of them were seriously smitten with the beauty of Lena Gray, the old Captain's only daughter, who had just come home from Smith College, with a certificate of graduation, five charming new hats, and a considerable knowledge of the art of amateur dramatics. She was cast for the part of leading lady in Samaria's play that summer, and Mr. Jones and Mr. Hopkins were both secretly ambitious for the post of stage-manager.

But it fell to Orlando Cutter, who lived on the farm next to the Grays. The disappointed candidates consoled themselves by the size of the bouquets which they threw to the heroine at the close of the third act. One was of white roses and red carnations; the other was of pink roses and lilies of the valley. The flowers that she carried when she answered the final curtain-call, curiously enough, were damask roses and mignonette. A minute observer would have noticed that there was a fine damask rose-bush growing in the Cutter's back garden.

There was no dispute of methods between Jones and Hopkins in the amatorial realm, like that which divided them in matters piscatorial. They were singularly alike in attitude and procedure. Both were very much in earnest; both expressed their earnestness by offerings presented to the object of their devotions; both hesitated to put their desires and hopes into words, because they could not do it in any but a serious way, and they feared to invite failure by a premature avowal. So, as I said, they stood in love upon an equal footing, but not an equality of success; rather one of doubt, delay and dissatisfaction. Miss Gray received their oblations with an admirable impartiality. She liked their books, their candy, their earnest conversation, their mild clerical jokes, without giving any indication which of them she liked best. As her father's daughter she was free from ecclesiastical entanglements; but of course she wanted to go to church, so she attended the Episcopal service at eleven o'clock and became a member of Mr. Hopkins's Bible Class which met at twelve thirty. Orlando Cutter usually drove home with her when the class was over.

You can imagine how eagerly and gravely Cotton Mather and Willibert considered the best means of advancing their respective wishes in regard to this young lady; how they sought for some gift which should not be too costly for her to accept with propriety, and yet sufficiently rare and distinguished to indicate her supreme place in their regards. They had sent her things to read and things to eat; they had drawn upon Hitchfield in the matter of flowers. Now each of them was secretly casting about in his mind for some unique thing to offer, which might stand out from trivial gifts, not by its cost, but by its individuality, by the impossibility of any other person's bringing it, and so might prepare the way for a declaration.

By a singular, yet not unnatural, coincidence, the solution presented itself to the imagination of each of them (separately and secretly of course) in the form of Leviathan.

I feel that a brief word of explanation is necessary here. Every New England village that has any trout-fishing in its vicinity has also a legend of a huge trout, a great-grandfather of fishes, præternaturally wise and wary, abnormally fierce and powerful, who lives in some particular pool of the principal stream, and is seen, hooked, and played by many anglers but never landed. Such a traditional trout there was at Samaria. His lair was in a deep hole of the Lirrapaug, beside an overhanging rock, and just below the mouth of the little spring-brook that divided the Gray's farm from the Cutter's. But this trout was not only traditional, he was also real. Small boys had fished for him, and described vividly the manner in which their hooks had been carried away,—but that does not count. Jags Witherbee declared that he had struggled with him for nearly an hour, only to fall exhausted in the rapids below the pool while the trout executed a series of somersaults in the direction of Simsville,—but that does not count. What really counts is that two reputable clergymen testified that they had seen him. He rose once to Jones's fly when he was fishing up the river after dusk, and Hopkins had seen him chase a minnow up the brook just before sunrise. The latter witness averred that the fish made a wake like a steamboat, and the former witness estimated his weight at a little short of five pounds,—both called him Leviathan, and desired to draw him out with a hook.

Now the thought that secretly occurred to each of these worthy young men, as I say, not unnaturally, but with a strange simultaneousness which no ordinary writer of fiction would dare to invent, was this: "Catch Leviathan on the last day of the trout-season and present him to Miss Gray. That will be a famous gift, and no one else can duplicate it."

The last day of the season was July 31st. Long before daybreak the Rev. Cotton Mather Hopkins stole away from the manse, slipping through the darkness noiselessly, and taking the steep path by Bushy Brook towards the valley of the Lirrapaug. In one pocket was his long, light, hand-line, carefully coiled, with a selected sneck-bend hook of tempered steel made fast to the line by the smallest and firmest of knots. In the other pocket was a box of choice angle-worms, dug from the garden two days before, and since that time kept in moss and sprinkled with milk to make them clean and rosy. It was his plan to go down stream a little way below the rock-pool, wait for daylight, and then fish up the pool slowly until he reached Leviathan's lair and caught him. It was a good plan.

The day came gently and serenely; a touch of gray along the eastern horizon; a fading of the deep blue overhead, a paling of the stars, a flush of orange in the east; then silver and gold on the little floating clouds, and amber and rose along the hill-tops; then lances of light showing over the edge of the world and a cool flood of diffused radiance flowing across field and river. It was at this moment, before there was a shadow to be found in the scene, that the bait-fisherman stepped into the rapid below the pool and began to wade slowly and cautiously upward along the eastern bank. Not a ripple moved before him; his steps fell on the rocky bottom as if he had been shod with velvet. The long line shot out from his swinging hand and the bait fell lightly on the pool,—too far away yet to reach the rock. Another cast follows, and still another, but without any result. The rock is now reached, but the middle of it pro-jects a little into the pool, and makes a bend or bay which is just out of sight from the point where the fisherman stands. He gathers his line in his left hand again and makes another cast. It is a beauty. The line uncoils itself without a hitch and the bait curves around the corner, settling down beside the rock as if a bit of sand had fallen from the top of the bank.

But what is that dark figure kneeling on the eastern bank at the head of the pool? It is the form of Willibert Beauchamp Jones, B.D. He has assumed this attitude of devotion in order that Leviathan may not see him from afar; but it also serves unconsciously to hide him from the fisherman at the foot of the pool. Willibert is casting the fly very beautifully, very delicately, very accurately, across the mouth of the spring-brook towards the upper end of the rock. The tiny royal coachman falls like a snowflake on the water, and the hare's ear settles like a bit of thistledown two feet beyond it. Nearer and nearer the flies come to the rock, until at last they cover the place where the last cast of the hand-line fell. There is a flash of purple and gold in the water, a great splash on the surface,—Leviathan has risen; Willibert has struck him; the royal coachman is fast in his upper lip.

At the same instant the fisherman at the

lower end of the pool feels a tightening of his line. He gives it a quick twitch with his right hand, and prepares to pull in with his left. Leviathan has taken the bait; Cotton Mather has struck; the hook is well fastened in the roof of the fish's mouth and the sport begins.

Willibert leaps to his feet and moves towards the end of the point. Cotton Mather, feeling the heavy strain on his line, wades out towards the deeper part of the pool. The two fishermen behold each other, in the moment of their common triumph, and they perceive what lies between them.

"Excuse me," said Hopkins, "but that is my fish. He must have taken my bait before he rose to the fly, and I'll be much obliged to you if you'll let go of him."

"I beg your pardon," replied Jones, "but it's quite evident that he rose to my fly before you felt him bite at your bait; and as I struck him first and hooked him first, he is my fish and I'll thank you to leave him alone."

It was a pretty situation. Each fisherman realized that he was called upon to do his best and yet unable to get ahead of the other without danger to his own success,—no time for argument surely! Yet I think they would have argued, and that with fierceness, had it not been for a sudden interruption.

"Good morning, gentlemen!" said the voice of Orlando Cutter, as he stepped from the bushes at the mouth of the brook, with a landing-net in his hand, "I see you are out early to-day. I came down myself to have a try for the big fish, and Miss Gray was good enough to come with me."

The rosy, laughing face of the girl emerged from the willows. "Good morning, good morning," she cried. "Why it's quite a party, isn't it? But how wet you both are, Mr. Hopkins and Mr. Jones,—did you fall in the water? And you look vexed, too! What is the matter? Oh, I see, both your lines are caught fast in the bottom of the pool,—no, they are tangled together"—(at this the fish gave a mighty splash and a rush towards the shore,)—"oh, Orlando, it's a fish, and such a beauty!"

The trout, bewildered and exhausted by the double strain upon him, floundered a little and moved into the shallow water at the mouth of the brook. Orlando stepped down and quietly slipped the landing-net under him.

"I see it is a fish," he said, "and it seems to be caught with a bait and a fly, but it certainly

is landed with a net. So in that case, gentlemen, as your claims seem to be divided, I will
take the liberty of disengaging both your hooks,
and of begging Miss Gray to accept this Leviathan, as—may I tell them?—she has just accepted me."

By this time the newly risen sun was shining
upon the ripples of the Lirrapaug River and
upon the four people who stood on the bank
shaking hands and exchanging polite remarks.
His glowing face was bright with that cheerful
air of humourous and sympathetic benevolence
with which he seems to look upon all our human
experiences of disappointment and success.

The weary anglers found some physical comfort, at least, in the cool glasses of milk which
Miss Gray poured for them as they sat on the
verandah of the farmhouse. On their way up
the hill, by the pleasant path which followed
Bushy Brook, these two brethren who were so
much of one mind in their devotion to their
fishing and who differed only in regard to the
method to be pursued, did not talk much, but
they felt themselves nearer to each other than
ever before. Something seemed to weave between them the delicate and firm bonds of a
friendship strengthened by a common aim and

chastened by a common experience of disappointment. They could afford to be silent together because they were now true comrades. I shall always maintain that both of them received a great benefit from Leviathan.

THE ART OF LEAVING OFF

THE ART OF LEAVING OFF

IT was a hot August Sunday, one of those days on which art itself must not be made too long lest it should shorten life. A little company of us had driven down from our hotel on the comparatively breezy hill to attend church in the village. The majority chose to pay their devotions at the big yellow meeting-house, where the preacher was reputed a man of eloquence; but my Uncle Peter drew me with him to the modest gray chapel, at the far end of the street, which was temporarily under the care of a student in the winter-school of theology, who was wisely spending his vacation in the summer-school of life. Some happy inspiration led the young man to select one of Lyman Abbott's shortest and simplest sermons,—itself a type of the mercy which it commended,—and frankly read it to us instead of pronouncing a discourse of his own. The result of this was that we came out of chapel at a quarter past eleven in a truly grateful and religious frame of mind.

But our comrades were still detained in the yellow meeting-house; and while the stage-coach waited for them in the glaring fervour of noon, my Uncle Peter and I climbed down from our seats and took refuge on the grass, in the shadow of the roundhead maples that stood guard along the north wall of the Puritan sanctuary. The windows were open. We could see the rhythmic motion of the fan-drill in the pews. The pulpit was not visible; but from that unseen eminence a strident, persistent voice flowed steadily, expounding the necessity and uses of "a baptism of fire," with a monotonous variety of application. Fire was needful for the young, for the middle-aged, for the old, and for those, if any, who occupied the intermediate positions. It was needful for the rich and for the poor, for the ignorant and for the learned, for church-members, for those who were "well-wishers" but not "professors," and for hardened sinners, —for everybody in fact: and if any class or condition of human creatures were omitted in the exhaustive analysis, the preacher led us to apprehend that he was only holding them in reserve, and that presently he would include them in the warm and triumphant application of his subject. He was one of those preachers who say it all, and make no demands upon the intelligence of their hearers.

Meantime the brown-and-yellow grasshoppers

crackled over the parched fields, and the locusts rasped their one-stringed fiddles in the trees, and the shrunken little river complained faintly in its bed, and all nature was sighing, not for fire, but for water and cool shade. But still the ardent voice continued its fuliginous exhortations, until the very fans grew limp, and the flowers in the hats of the village girls seemed to wilt with fervent heat.

My Uncle Peter and I were brought up in that old-fashioned school of manners which discouraged the audible criticism of religious exercises. But we could not help thinking.

"He has just passed 'Secondly,'" said I, "and that leaves two more main heads, and a practical conclusion of either three or five points."

My Uncle Peter said nothing in answer to this. After a while he remarked in an abstract, disconnected way: "I wonder why no school of divinity has ever established a professorship of the Art of Leaving Off."

"The thing is too simple," I replied; "theological seminaries do not concern themselves with the simplicities."

"And yet," said he, "the simplest things are often the most difficult and always the most important. The proverb says that 'well begun is half done.' But the other half is harder and more necessary,—to get a thing well ended. It is the final word that is most effective, and it is something quite different from the last word. Many a talker, in the heat of his discussion and his anxiety to have the last word, runs clear past the final word and never gets back to it again."

"Talking," said I, "is only a small part of life, and not of much consequence."

"I don't agree with you," he answered. "The tongue is but a little member, yet behold how great a fire it kindles. Talking, rightly considered, is the expression and epitome of life itself. All the other arts are but varieties of talking. And in this matter of the importance of the final touch, the point at which one leaves off, talking is just a symbol of everything else that we do. It is the last step that costs, says the proverb; and I would like to add, it is the last step that counts."

"Be concrete," I begged, "I like you best that way."

"Well," he continued, "take the small art of making artificial flies for fishing. The knot that is hardest to tie is that which finishes off the confection, and binds the feathers and the silk securely to the hook, gathering up the loose ends and concealing them with invisible firmness. I remember, when I first began to tie flies, I never could arrive at this final knot, but kept on and on, winding the thread around the hook and making another half-hitch to fasten the ones that were already made, until the alleged fly looked like a young ostrich with a sore throat.

"Or take the art of sailing a boat. You remember Fanny Adair? She had a sublime confidence in herself that amounted to the first half of genius. She observed that, given a wind and a sail and a rudder, any person of common sense could make a boat move along. So she invited a small party of equally inexperienced friends to go out with her in a cat-boat on Newport harbour. The wind was blowing freshly and steadily towards the wharf, and neither the boat-keeper nor I suspected any lack in Fanny's competence as she boldly grasped the tiller and started out in fine style, beating merrily to and fro across the bay. I went up town and came back at the appointed hour of six o'clock to meet the party. The wind was still blowing freshly and steadily, straight onto the wharf, but they had not returned. They were beating up and down, now skimming near to the landing, now darting away from it. We called them to come in. I saw a look of desperation settle on Fanny's face. She slacked away the main-sheet, put the boat before the wind, held the tiller straight, and ran down upon the wharf with a crash that cracked the mast and tumbled the passengers over like ten-pins in a strike. 'I knew I could sail the old thing,' said Fanny, 'but I didn't think it would be so hard to stop her!'"

"I see what you mean," said I. "Isn't the same difficulty often experienced by after-dinner speakers and lecturers, and speculators on the stock-market, and moral reformers, and academic co-ordinators of the social system of the universe?"

"It is," he answered. "They can sail the sea of theory splendidly, but they don't know how to make a landing. Yet that is really the thing that everybody ought to learn. No voyage is successful unless you deliver the goods. Even in a pleasure-voyage there must be a fit time and place for leaving off. There is a psychological moment at which the song has made its most thrilling impression, and there the music should cease. There is an instant of persuasion at which the argument has had its force, and there it should break off, just when the nail is driven home, and before the hammer begins to bruise the wood. The art lies in discovering this moment of cessation and using it to the best advantage. That is the fascination of the real 'short story' as told by Hawthorne, or Poe, or Stevenson, or Cable, or De Maupassant, or Miss Jewett, or Margaret Deland. It reaches the point of interest and stops. The impression is not blurred. It is like a well-cut seal: small, but clear and sharp. You take the imprint of it distinctly. Stockton's story of 'The Lady or the Tiger' would not gain anything by an addition on the natural history of tigers or the psychological peculiarities of ladies.

"That is what is meant by the saying that 'brevity is the soul of wit,'—the thing that keeps it alive. A good joke prolonged degenerates into teasing; and a merry jest with explanations becomes funereal. When a man repeats the point of his story it is already broken off. Somebody said of Mr. Gladstone's oratory that it was 'good, but copious.' Canaries sing well, but the defect of their music is its abundance. I prefer the hermit-thrush to the nightingale, not because the thrush's notes are sweeter, but because he knows when to leave off, and let his song vanish, at the exquisite moment, into the silence of mysterious twilight."

"You seem to be proving," I said, "what most men will admit without argument, that 'enough is as good as a feast.'"

"On the contrary," he replied, "I am arguing against that proverb. Enough is not as good as a feast. It is far better. There is something magical and satisfying in the art of leaving off. Good advice is infinitely more potent when it is brief and earnest than when it dribbles into vague exhortations. Many a man has been worried into vice by well-meant but wearisome admonitions to be virtuous. A single word of true friendly warning or encouragement is more eloquent than volumes of nagging pertinacity, and may safely be spoken and left to do its work. After all when we are anxious to help a friend into the right path, there is not much more or better that we can say than what Sir Walter Scott said, when he was a-dying, to his son-in-law Lockhart: 'Be a good man, my dear, be a good man.' The life must say the rest."

"You are talking as seriously," said I, "as if you were a preacher and we were in a church."

"Are we not?" said he, very quietly. "When we are thinking and talking of the real meaning of life it seems to me that we are in the Temple. Let me go on a moment longer with my talk. We often fancy, in this world, that beautiful and pleasant things would satisfy us better if they could be continued, without change, for-

THE ART OF LEAVING OFF

ever. We regret the ending of a good 'day off.' We are sorry to be 'coming out of the woods' instead of 'going in.' And that regret is perfectly natural and all right. It is part of the condition on which we receive our happiness. The mistake lies in wishing to escape from it by a petrification of our joys. The stone forest in Arizona will never decay, but it is no place for a man to set up his tents forever.

"The other day, a friend was admiring the old-fashioned house where I live. ''Tis *a good camp*,' said I, 'plenty of wood and water, and I hope it's on the right trail.'

"Many of our best friends have gone ahead of us on that trail. Why should we hold back? The fairest things in the world and the finest are always in transition: the bloom of tender Spring disappearing in the dark verdure of Summer; the week of meadow-rue and nodding lilies passing as silently as it came; the splendid hues of the autumnal hills fading like the colours on a bubble; the dear child, whose innocence and simplicity are a daily joy to you, growing up into a woman. Would you keep her a child forever, her head always a little lower than your heart? Would you stand where you are to-day, always doing the same things, always repeating the same experiences, never leaving off? Then be thankful that the Wisdom and Goodness by which this passing show is ordered will not suffer you to indulge your foolish wish. The wisest men and women are not those who cling tenaciously to one point of life, with desperate aversion to all change, but those who travel cheerfully through its mutations, finding in every season, in every duty, in every pleasure, a time to begin and a time to cease, and moving on with willing adaptation through the conclusion of each chapter to the end of the book.

"And concerning that *Finis* of the volume, which is printed in such sober, black, italic type, I remember a good saying of old Michel de Montaigne in one of his essays,—not the exact words, but the soul of his remarks. He says that we cannot judge whether a man has been truly fortunate in life until we have seen him act with tranquillity and contentment in the last scene of his comedy, which is undoubtedly the most difficult. For himself, he adds, his chief study and desire is that he may well behave himself at his last gasp, that is quietly and constantly. It is a good saying; for life has no finer lesson to teach us than how to leave off."

"I wish you would promise me one thing,"

292

said I to my Uncle Peter: "that you will not leave off before I do."

"Ah," he answered, "that is the one thing that no man can promise another. We can promise not to break friendship, not to cut loose, not to cease loving, not to forget. Isn't that enough?"

He stood up reverently and bared his head. The music of the long-metre doxology was floating through the open windows.

"Listen," he said. "If that is true, what more do we need? We are all in His hand."

www.ingramcontent.com/pod-product-compliance
Lightning Source LLC
Chambersburg PA
CBHW030937260626
47169CB00002B/512